Fogging Over

Fogging Over

ANNIE DALTON

An imprint of HarperCollins*Publishers*

With thanks to Australian angels Kerry Greenwood and Jenny Pausacker for helping me with Mel's trip to the Northern Territories. Thanks also to Viv French for helping me find my way round Victorian London. And a special thank you to my daughter Maria for her totally luminous inspiration!

First published in Great Britain by Collins in 2002

Collins is an imprint of HarperCollins*Publishers* Ltd,
77–85 Fulham Palace Road, Hammersmith,
London, W6 8JB

1 3 5 7 9 10 8 6 4 2

The HarperCollins website address is:
www.fireandwater.com

Text copyright © Annie Dalton 2002

The author asserts the moral right to be
identified as the author of this work.

ISBN 0 00 712987 4

Printed and bound in England by
Clays Ltd, St Ives plc

CHAPTER ONE

Once upon a time, I lived on a gorgeous blue-green planet called Earth. I didn't stay long, thirteen years and twenty-two hours max. But it often felt a whole lot longer. That's because I was in a perpetual state of panic. It would take too long to list all the things I was scared of. There were all the normal human anxieties obviously: spiders, dentists, exams. Plus those typical teen twitches, worrying that I looked fat or had evil-smelling breath or that I'd been walking around the school with my skirt trapped in my knickers. These were just my background worries! The bass line for the heavy stuff.

But one fear was so humiliating that I never admitted it to anybody.

I was petrified of being by myself. I knew it was nuts, even at the time. Loneliness can't actually kill you, right? But the minute I was alone, I literally felt myself dissolving with terror. My home felt SO empty. Even with the TV on full blast. Even when I called my mates and kept them talking for hours on the phone. Even if I made butterscotch-flavoured popcorn and pigged the lot. Even – well, you get the picture.

It all started when my dad walked out. Naturally I started worrying that Mum would be next to abandon me. Every time she left the flat, I knew she was going to get mashed in a road accident and I'd be taken into care. But she didn't and I wasn't, and eventually she met my lovely stepdad Des. After we all moved in together I let myself relax for a whole twenty-four hours. Ohh, it was bliss! But next day, EEP! I was back on Red Alert. Only now I was panicking about Des dying in the same tragic car wreck. Plus a few months later, my baby sister was born, so then I had to add her to my panic list too.

But that's all ancient history. These days you'll find me living happily on the other side of those famous Pearly Gates. I know! Unbelievable isn't it? It was actually me who died, which is about the one scenario that never occurred to me! I just wish I could go on *Oprah* and broadcast an inspirational message to the stressed-out Mel Beebys of this world.

"Go with the flow, babes," I'd tell them. "No matter what happens, you can handle it. You're ALL going to be fine!" And to prove it, I'd show them some feel-good footage from my personal video diary.

To a cool hip hop soundtrack, you see this like, MTV montage of me and my mates, shopping in our favourite department stores, paddling on the seashore and dancing the night away at the Babylon Café. At the end I'm by myself. The camera pulls back to show my friend Lola Sanchez watching as I sashay through the school gates. "At first glance, Melanie Beeby looks like any normal schoolgirl," she tells the viewer. "But appearances can be deceptive and this is no ordinary school."

The camera focuses on a sign saying *Angel Academy* in shimmery letters, then zooms in on the angel logo on the gates. Next minute there's a new close-up of the identical logo, only this one is on my cute midriff T-shirt. I go floating through the school in graceful slow-mo, chatting and laughing with my mates.

Then CUT! Lola and I are sipping strawberry smoothies at Guru, our favourite student hang-out.

"I used to think of death as the ultimate tragedy," I confide in my friend. "Like this scary black hole that swallowed you up for ever? But the fact is, dying totally improved my life. Naturally I was upset to leave my family," I add hastily. "But at my old school I'd got this reputation for being a real bimbo. One teacher called me 'an airhead with attitude'."

Lola pulls a face into the camera. "Yeah, Miss Rowntree!" she says cheekily. "And look at her now!"

"I was so amazed when I got to Heaven and found I'd won a scholarship to the Angel Academy!" I giggle. "Someone must have thought I had hidden depths!"

Now Lola and I are walking past the school library. It's made of glass and looks a bit like a lighthouse, only with magic cloud effects scudding over the walls.

"We don't think of ourselves as pupils," I say into the camera. "We're trainees. And if we make the grade we'll be the celestial agents of the future, which has to be the coolest job ever."

The scene dissolves, and we're in the middle of a science class. Mr Allbright is demonstrating a new technique for beaming celestial vibes. After a few attempts, everyone successfully materialises a wobbly sphere of golden light above his or her cupped palms. We all look v. intellectual, especially Lola, who's wearing cute little gold glasses.

This time it's my voice on the soundtrack. "Lollie is my best friend," I tell the world happily. "She's the soul-mate I've been longing for my whole life, which is incredible as originally she's from my future! Angel trainees can come from every period of Earth's history. Oh, except for pure angels like my buddy Reuben here."

The camera drops in on a martial arts class, where a skinny, honey-coloured boy is performing a sequence of ninja angel moves. He looks focused, yet v. endearing with his little dreads whipping around his head.

CUT! It's sunset and the whole class is sitting on the beach in the lotus position. The sun slips down into the ocean, beaming rosy rays across our faces. A musical throbbing builds on the soundtrack, sounding like some huge divine humming top.

I say, "This is the first sound I heard after I left my body and found myself in Heaven. I call it my cosmic lullaby, because it makes me feel really safe and secure. You see, life really doesn't end when you die! The truth is, it just gets better and better!"

At this point though, my video diary totally runs out of steam.

Diaries are meant to tell the truth and I'm not sure mine is giving a true picture. Perhaps you didn't notice, but in trying to focus on the bright side, I accidentally make my school look like a Pepsi commercial. Like, I never *once* mention the Dark Powers. I also give the impression that I'm finally sorted (yeah, right!).

But like our teacher says, being an angel is not about being perfect. It's about being real. So I want you to forget all about that phony Pepsi Heaven, because I'm about to tell you the uncut, unvarnished, totally unglamorous story of my last assignment.

But first, to help you understand what happened, I've got to tell you about Brice.

I ran into Brice on my very first trouble-shooting mission to Earth. At that time he was working for the PODS (that's what my mates and I call the Powers of Darkness). I won't lie to you, I hated him on sight. It didn't help that this cosmic low-life was the exact double of a really buff boy I once fancied at my old school, right down to the bleached hair and bad-boy slouch.

Anyway, without going into the sordid details, I got the better of him. After that Brice became like, my evil nemesis or whatever, because he turned up again on our mission to Tudor England. This time he beat our buddy Reuben up so badly that Reubs had to be airlifted back home. He's still got a huge scar.

Now I've convinced you that Brice belongs firmly on the dark side of the cosmic fence, right? Unfortunately, it's not that simple.

You see, once upon a time, Brice was an angel like me.

I know, it's too disturbing for words. I don't understand why it seems more shocking for a Light Worker to go over to the Opposition than if he'd been bad from the beginning, but it does.

I'm not going to get into why Brice sold his soul to the PODS. But the Agency obviously believed there were extenuating circumstances, because last term, after complex negotiations with the Opposition (that's the official Agency term for the Dark Powers), they brought Brice in from the cold. And next thing I know, bosh! He's back at school. They actually had him working on the Guardian Angel hotline, would you believe!

Our headmaster explained that the Agency has to take the long-term view. He also said a heap of other stuff, about Eternity and how if you wait long enough trees sometimes evolve into diamonds. It was an excellent speech, but I still thought Brice was a jerk.

Luckily he was keeping totally out of my way. I'd catch glimpses of him at various student hang-outs, but he was always on his own and never stayed longer than a few minutes. Once I bumped into him mooching around the stacks in the school library. And another time I saw him on the beach, chucking pebbles at the sea, looking incredibly depressed.

The boy's a freak, I thought smugly. He can't hack the Hell dimensions and he can't stand Heaven. I bet he won't make it to the end of term.

Basically I couldn't wait for Brice to let everyone down again and go slinking back to the Opposition. Then I could pretend the creep never existed and life could go back to how it was before.

Then summer came and things took a totally unexpected turn.

I only have myself to blame for what happened. Lola was desperate for me to spend the holidays with her, in the heavenly interior doing adventure activities. "Everyone says you come back totally transformed," she enthused. "We'll be like angel warriors! The PODS won't know what hit them!"

But I'm not the bungee-jumping type, and anyway I'd promised to help out at the preschoolers' summer camp. So at the end of term, we went our separate ways.

For the first few days I literally felt like I was missing a limb.

Every time I went into town I'd leave a message for Lollie on the Link – the angel internet. But days and weeks went by and she still didn't reply.

I told myself she must be holidaying somewhere remote, where they hadn't even heard of internet cafés. But I wasn't convinced. I mean, we're both angels, right? Normally I know the instant she's thinking about me. Yet I was getting this permanently 'ENGAGED' signal, as if my soul-mate's thoughts had drifted totally elsewhere.

Luckily with thirty hyperactive angel tots to take care of, I didn't have time to mope. Days whizzed by in a blur of activity: picnics on the beach, treasure hunts among the dunes, trips to the Sugar Shack for home-made ices. Until finally it was our last day. Since we'd worked so hard, Miss Dove told us we could have a couple of hours off.

Picture me lying in a hammock in the afternoon sunshine, listening to the soothing whisper of waves from the beach below, my eyes glued to a spine-chilling novel I'd found in our holiday cottage. From nearby came a babble of excited little voices as the toddlers tried to guess the mystery objects in Miss Dove's special magic bag.

I heard the creak of a hammock and Amber sat up. "Boy, you've really got the bug," she yawned. You were reading Sherlock Holmes last time I looked!"

"Finished it last night," I mumbled.

My reading marathon started out of sheer self defence. After a hard day keeping up with the tinies, I needed to flake out and relax. Unfortunately Amber and the other volunteers were bursting to hold lengthy midnight discussions on various deep angelic issues. I didn't want to hurt their feelings, so I had to pretend to be fascinated by the mildewed book collection in my attic bedroom. I guess I must have been quite bored, because one book led to another and I was now shamelessly addicted – my current read had me totally mesmerised! You would not *believe* the things that happened to that heroine. First both her parents die in a storm at sea. Then her relatives pack her off to a typhoid-ridden boarding school on the moors, so they can cheat her out of her rightful inheritance. I was desperate to know how it would turn out.

Suddenly shrieks of excitement made me look up.

"YAYY!! I guessed right!" Next minute little Maudie landed on top of me. My hammock wobbled madly, tipping both of us on the ground, and I found myself buried under a heap of giggling preschool angels.

But finally the day was over and my fellow volunteers and I tottered back to our cottage at the top of the cliffs. It was still really warm so we ate outdoors, watching the lighthouse wink on and off across the bay.

Out of the blue, Amber said, "So have you guys decided where you're going yet?"

For the second time that day I came back to reality with a bump.

"Omigosh!" I gasped. "I can't believe I forgot!"

Mr Allbright had announced that the History students would be going on a field trip at the beginning of the new term; a trip with a twist. We had to pick an era in human history which interested us. If the Agency approved, we'd be assigned a suitable human from that time period and we'd go to Earth to study them in their natural context.

That's what I think is SO cool about my school. We don't just learn history from books, we visit historical eras for real. I'm serious, we literally travel in Time!

This time we were supposed to be working in groups of three, something to do with power triangles or whatever. I naturally assumed I'd be in a three with my fellow cosmic musketeers, Lollie and Reuben. But it had been a v. stressful term and my frazzled mates couldn't seem to agree on anything.

Lola had insisted we went back to ancient Persia where she'd done her Guardian Angel module. And Reuben had this bizarre fixation with King Arthur and his Round Table.

"I hate to burst your bubble, hon," I said, "but the King Arthur thing is just a story. Camelot never actually existed."

As a pure angel Reuben often finds it hard to grasp quite basic concepts, such as the difference between human history and fairy tales. In the end my mates grumpily informed me that they'd leave our destination entirely up to moi. And I'd immediately put it to the back of my mind. After all, I had the whole summer in front of me.

Only now the holidays were over and I still hadn't thought of a destination. You see, I wanted it to be somewhere truly amazing. I mean, I wanted my mates to have a great time, but most of all I wanted to wow them with my super de luxe five-star decision-making. Unfortunately under that kind of pressure my mind turns to pink bubblegum, incapable of making even weedy one-star decisions!

Yikes! I wasn't even back at school yet but my stress levels were soaring dangerously. So I took myself off to have a calming read in the bath.

I lit a small army of candles, climbed into the old-fashioned tub, lay back in the hot water and settled down to finish my mystery. The pages started going wavy in the steam, but I refused to budge until the evil rellies got their just desserts. At last I closed the book with a sigh of satisfaction. Then I shot bolt upright, sending bath foam everywhere. I'd had the most fantabulous idea!

I towelled myself dry, put on my cute *Treat me like a Princess* T-shirt and flew into my room to investigate my antique book collection.

Every title gave me goosebumps! *The Story of Dr Jekyll and Mr Hyde*, *The Woman in White*, *Collected Ghost Stories* by Charles Dickens, and most spine-tingling of all, real-life reports of the case of Jack the Ripper! And all these books were written in the exact same era. Victorian times. Well, was that a sign, or was that a sign?

I grabbed the Ripper book and screwed my eyes tight shut. "Just give me a date," I muttered. "Any date will do." I opened the book at random and peeped out from under my lashes.

There it was, bang in the middle of the page. 1888!

By total fluke, I'd found the perfect destination for our time trip. Lola, Reubs and I could do a spot of enjoyable time-tourism, plus we'd collect enough info on social conditions and whatever to satisfy our teacher.

Now I could relax and enjoy the last few hours of my holiday with a clear conscience. I was so impressed with myself, it never occurred to me that my mates might not be as thrilled with my idea as I was!

Have you noticed how the moments you most look forward to are so often the ones that are a total let-down?

The instant I got back to school, I hurtled along to Lollie's room to tell her the good news, but she still hadn't returned from her adventure holiday. So I dashed along to my room and called Reuben's number. Reuben *had* to be back. Only he wasn't.

I collapsed on to my narrow bed and gazed out over the heavenly rooftops. It was evening and lights were coming on all over the city, like sprinkles of little stars. But tonight this beauty just made me feel depressed. "Hi, I'm back," I told my empty room. And then I said, "Well, can't sit about here all day."

I unpacked my bags, singing along to my current fave single, a sweet little hip hop track called *True Colours*. After that, I had a shower, drying and conditioning my hair slowly and carefully. And after that, I gave my little orange tree some overdue TLC, lovingly polishing every leaf with Leaf Shine. But there was still no sign of Lola.

"I'll lie down for a minute," I told myself. "I won't go to sleep. I'll just rest my eyes."

But the next thing I knew, my room was full of dazzling celestial sunlight. Someone had posted a message under my door while I was sleeping. With a rush of happiness I recognised Lola's handwriting.

Yo! Sleeping Beauty! We're having breakfast at Guru to celebrate our last hour of freedom!
Big love,
Lollie xxx

My soul-mate was back in town!

Guru's chef must have been making their special chocolate brownies when I arrived, because the café smelled divine.

I heard a husky chuckle and spotted my friend's mad dark curls over by the window. She was chatting to some real outdoor types, looking incredibly pretty in a cute red dress I'd never seen before.

Pure happiness fizzed up inside me. I planned to sneak up and put my hands over her eyes. Ta da!

Before I could reach her, Brice burst through the kitchen doors, waving a bottle of maple syrup. "Here you are, princess! You can't eat pancakes without maple syrup." He sat down beside her, draping an arm round the back of her chair.

I couldn't believe what I was seeing.

"This isn't happening!" I whispered. But it was.

My best friend and my old enemy were an item.

Chapter Two

I wanted to run but I was totally paralysed. Anyway, it was too late – Lola had already spotted me.

"Boo!" she shrieked. "Omigosh! I've missed you so much!"

I have no idea why Lola calls me Boo. She loves giving her friends crazy nicknames.

Lola poked Brice in the ribs. "Don't just sit there, you monster! Find her a chair!"

My soul-mate seemed to think everything was quite normal. Like, "It's no big deal. I've just spent my entire holidays with a cosmic juvenile delinquent."

Well, it *was* a big deal. I was completely

traumatised. So much so that I behaved like a complete child, blanking Brice and babbling to my friend as if we were alone.

"Guess what, babe!" I wittered. "I had this brilliant idea for Mr Allbright's time project. And I'm thinking Victorian times, because they—"

"That's great," Lola said politely. "Though I have to tell you, after the summer we've had, schoolwork seems kind of irrelevant. Oh, Mel, I wish you'd come with us! We had such a fabulous time, didn't we?" She beamed at Brice. "You should have seen us canoeing down that waterfall, babe! Omigosh, those canoes are SO tiny, I don't know how we both—"

"OK, tell me the details later," I said hastily. "Look, about that project—"

"You've got to come with us next time!" Lola interrupted. "It's SO sublime. We used to take our sleeping bags outside and just lie staring up at the stars. Oh, but one night, something really funny happened." Lollie gave her husky chuckle. "It makes me laugh just thinking about it!"

Just then Reuben came in. Unlike me, Reuben has a forgiving nature. So when he saw our best friend openly sharing maple syrup with the thug who'd put him in the hospital, he didn't seem to think anything of it. Brice also seemed to think it was all water under the bridge.

"Have my seat, mate," he told Reuben. "They're expecting me down at the Agency."

"Why? Got an appointment with your probation officer?" I said spitefully.

Brice just blew me a kiss on his way out.

Good riddance, I thought. Lola had started chatting to someone else about her holiday, but I didn't want to hear about her and Brice gazing up at the stars, so I hooked my arm through Reuben's. "Reubs, I was just telling Lola about this idea I had for our project."

"Melanie!" he protested. "I just got back five minutes ago!"

"I know, babe, but they're expecting us at the Agency any minute and they'll ask us where we're going, so you've got to back me up and say we want to go to London in 1888."

"Why, what's so special about 1888?"

"Oh, loads of stuff," I said enthusiastically, to cover the fact that my mind had gone embarrassingly blank.

"Name one," he insisted.

"Well, erm – for one thing, Jack the Ripper was still stalking the streets!" I remembered triumphantly.

"Doing what?" Reuben couldn't have looked less impressed.

"Duh! Murdering people, what else!"

My angel buddy shook his head. "I don't get it."

"Oh come on," I groaned. "The Ripper has to be the most famous serial killer in history."

Reuben's expression went from blank, to confused, to totally appalled. "You're kidding? They made someone famous because he *murdered* people?"

I took a deep breath, reminding myself that Reuben often finds it hard to understand human behaviour. "I suppose it's because he was never caught," I explained. "It makes him seem immortal, kind of. Like he's still out there somewhere."

"But that's really sick."

"Well, don't blame me," I said defensively. "It's history, OK! You can't just pick out the pretty bits."

"Whatever," said Reuben. "Anyway, you'll have to count me out. I promised I'd help Chase with this tiger conservation thing."

I was genuinely shocked. I couldn't believe Reubs was ducking out.

"But you have to come!" I wailed. "Mr Allbright said we had to work in threes!"

"Then find someone else." Reuben glanced at

his watch. "We'd better run. We're due down at the Agency in five minutes."

The Agency, if you hadn't guessed, is the angelic organisation which keeps the whole of Creation running smoothly, so the Agency building is kind of Angel HQ.

There are gorgeous buildings everywhere in this city, but the Agency Tower is truly fabulous. Sometimes I get the feeling it's alive. It's made of special stuff that changes colour constantly. And with that high-level cosmic activity going on inside, you feel the vibes when you're still like, streets away.

On the way downtown, Reuben and Lola swapped holiday stories, but I didn't join in. Helping at a preschool camp doesn't exactly compare with canoeing down waterfalls or saving tigers. And anyway, they were meant to be my best friends and they had totally let me down.

We went in through the revolving doors, flashed our IDs at the guy on the desk, and took the lift up to the floor where we have our Agency briefings.

Trainees were already crowding into the hall, and I lost my mates in the crush. I spotted Orlando in front of me and felt a blush creeping up my neck.

Officially Orlando still goes to our school. Unofficially, he does a lot of hush-hush assignments for the Agency. Orlando's a genius basically – not a twisted genius like Brice, the real thing. Ohh, and he is SO cute! He literally looks like an angel; the gorgeous kind you see in old Italian paintings.

Hmmn, I thought. Maybe I could persuade dishy Orlando to be in our three? I was just about to take the plunge when Lola came dashing up.

"Boo, I'm so sorry! I didn't have my school head on back there," she said breathlessly. "Look, I trust you, OK. I'm sure we'll have a great time in 1880 or whenever, and don't worry about Reuben dropping out. It's all sorted!"

"It is?" I said.

"Totally. I told Brice and he insisted on taking Reuben's place. Isn't that SO sweet!"

"Well, actually," I croaked. "I don't know if I—"

"Mel, relax. It'll be great! Brice has changed. He really has!" She beamed into my eyes.

But I wasn't sure I wanted to go to Jack the Ripper's London any more. Especially not if I had to go with Brice.

Then I suddenly saw how this could work out to my advantage.

Right now Lola was seeing Brice through a holiday glow, which was partly my fault. I hadn't been around to give her regular reality checks, which is what good mates are for, right?

But if the three of us went on the same time trip, the cracks would start to show, and she'd have to see him for the charmless yob he really was. OK, this might not be much fun for Lola, but she'd thank me in the end.

"That sounds like a fabulous idea," I said brightly. "Let's sign up!"

We joined one of the queues of trainees, waiting to register their choice of destination with junior members of staff. Yet again I found myself wondering why all the younger agents look so poker-faced. Would it kill them to smile once in a while?

The agent looked startled when I told him our destination, but he dutifully typed our data into his laptop and said it would take an hour to match us with a suitable human.

I was going to suggest that Lola and I spent the time shopping for new outfits. But before I could get the words out, Brice came schmoozing up, and Lola said apologetically, "Oh Mel, you don't mind do you? I said I'd help Brice find some new jeans." And before I could say, "Actually, I do mind," the two of them headed out of the door hand in hand.

I stared after them. Don't over-react babe, I told myself shakily. Lola is a very tactile person. She'll hold hands with anyone. It doesn't mean a thing. There is no reason for your feelings to be hurt.

Luckily I remembered how in magazine advice columns they tell you to do something v. positive for yourself, so I took myself into town for a spot of v. positive retail therapy. And guess what! I went into The Source and found the most delicious little vintage top which would give my hipster jeans and boots the perfect retro twist.

But when I walked back into the Agency Tower, I couldn't believe my eyes. My soul-mate was waiting for the lift, wearing an identical top to mine! We stared at each other. "How totally luminous!" she screamed. "You got the same one!"

I went weak with relief. This was ultimate proof that Lola and I are spiritual twins, which meant that nothing and no-one could ever come between us.

"Where's Brice?" I asked casually.

"Still shopping," she said. "I've been telling him he should get some new stuff. His old clothes kind of smell."

"Oh, right," I said politely.

Lollie wrinkled her nose. "Yeah, some of the Hell dimensions are really whiffy, and it doesn't wash out apparently. Anyway, fill me in on these Victorians, *carita*! Michael is sure to ask questions."

By the time Michael buzzed us in, Brice still hadn't turned up, which put me in a real quandary. On the one hand I wanted Lola to know what a scumbag he was. But if he let us down, our Victorian trip would have to be called off.

Suddenly he came panting along the corridor.

"You're late," I said.

"No, sweetie, you're early. I'm totally on time."

I was going to tell him where to get off, but Lola said quickly, "You got that Diesel top after all. It looks great on you."

Brice looked down at his grey hoodie as if he had no idea where it had come from. "What, this?"

"Come on, you guys, Michael's waiting."

I was genuinely shocked when I first got here and heard all the kids referring to our headmaster by his first name. But I soon discovered that Michael is not your average headmaster. In fact he's an archangel, one of the immortal beings who oversee the running of Creation. The poor sweetheart has permanent jetlag from zipping between Earth's major trouble spots. But no matter how tired he is, Michael is totally with the programme. And when he looks at me with those scary beautiful archangel eyes, it's like he literally sees into my soul.

As usual he went straight to the point. "I won't deny that I was slightly concerned at your choice of era. I gather it was your idea, Mel, and I wasn't sure you'd realised all the implications?"

I'd been thinking the same thing, but now Michael had put it into words I felt really offended. He thinks I can't hack it, I thought, but I hid my hurt feelings with a little airhead joke. "No way are we backing out," I giggled. "We might get to meet Sherlock Holmes!"

"Hate to shatter your illusions, sweetheart," Brice murmured, "but Holmes was a fictional character."

I gave him my most poisonous look. "I did know that, actually."

Michael was constructing miniature steeples with his fingers. "I felt much better when I heard you were going to be the third member of the team," he said to Brice. "I seem to remember you spent some time in this era."

Brice just nodded expressionlessly. I guessed this was some oblique reference to his murky PODS past.

"I'll be frank," Michael said. "If it wasn't for you, I'd be asking the girls to reconsider. But if you're going along, I know they'll be in experienced hands."

Oh, this is great, I thought. Not only had my enemy been reinstated in Heaven, now I was meant to look up to him for his dodgy past!

Michael began shuffling the papers on his desk, a sign our interview was coming to an end. "This is an ideal opportunity for you to understand what makes this era tick. But as you know, some eras are especially tough to handle, so try to stay centred and alert, won't you? I'm expecting you to take good care of them," he said to Brice.

He flushed. "I'll do my best."

I gave Michael my sweetest smile. "Oh, we'll be fine! We're big girls now."

As usual, the Departures area was a hive of mad activity. We queued for our angel tags, then we queued all over again for our Agency watches, then we had to hang about waiting for the maintenance staff to finish servicing our portal. But finally we stepped inside and the glass door slid shut.

I always get serious butterflies at this point and no wonder. We were going to be blasted from a world of divine beauty and harmony into the bubbling stewpot of History. Lola normally relieves the tension by singing the tune Reuben wrote for us. It starts, "You're not alone, you're not alone," and it always makes me feel better. But today she seemed to forget about our little departure ritual. She just kept glancing nervously at Brice, like, "Oh, I hope he'll be OK." He seemed totally oblivious, listening to his headset.

So I sang our theme tune to myself in my head. "You're not alone, You're not alone." I kept on singing it until we took off.

The portal lit up in a blue-white blaze of cosmic light, and the heavenly city fell away as we blasted through the invisible barrier which divides the angelic fields from the beautiful unpredictable fields of Space and Time.

Centuries of history flew past in minutes, making gorgeous coloured patterns in the dark. As we drew closer to our time zone, the colours grew more and more intense. This time we made an impressively smooth landing. The portal door slid back and we stepped on to my favourite planet. Or rather, we floated.

I stared around me in shock. "What in the world—?"

We were in a desert so red it seemed to glow. The vegetation was like nothing on Earth. Spiky bushes with pink berries that looked fake. Stunted trees with pale papery leaves. A flock of birds flew past, their marshmallow-pink feathers perfectly matching the waxy pink berries. All the birds landed on the same branch, chuckling to themselves like birds in a cartoon.

The desert air smelled scorched and deeply alien, like I imagine it might smell on Mars. Perhaps it *was* Mars. That would explain the surprising lack of gravity.

Brice blew out his breath. "All right, I give up. Anyone know what we're doing in Australia?"

"Australia?" I gulped. "Are you serious?"

The pink cartoon birds suddenly decided to turn themselves the wrong way up. They just hung there, chuckling, letting the blood rush to their heads.

"I think those are galah birds," said Brice. "And the trees are definitely eucalyptus. So somewhere in the Northern Territories is my guess."

"But it feels so strange," said Lola. "I feel like I could just float away."

"Me too," I agreed.

Even our voices sounded floaty, like voices in a dream.

"The Agency must have miscalculated," I said in my floaty voice. "We'd better call them so they can get us back on track."

Brice shook his head. "They don't make that kind of mistake."

"But Michael agreed we could go to Victorian London," I protested childishly.

"So? For some reason they wanted us to come here first."

"But why would they send us somewhere uninhabited?"

Brice sighed. "This land is not uninhabited, sweetheart. Aborigines live here for one thing. Plus there's a road." He pointed through the shimmering heat haze.

"I'd call that a track," I said sniffily.

"Call it what you like. People made it and people use it. All kinds of people. Herders looking for work on cattle stations, missionaries looking for converts, hunters, trappers, telegraph workers—"

I was just wishing I had something to throw at him when I heard rustling and panting sounds. A demented-looking figure came stumbling through the bush. For a minute I actually thought it might be a mirage, but suddenly he gave this heart-rending cry, "Someone help me!" Then he crumpled across the track and went totally still.

We went skimming over to him, our feet barely touching the ground. I'd have worried about this normally, but we had a human emergency to attend to.

I stared down at the wild old man and felt myself shiver.

Something terrible had happened to him. I don't mean just physically. He was like those trees you see that have been struck by lightning, all blasted and hollow inside.

I saw a tiny muscle move in Brice's cheek. "Poor guy must have got close to the PODS."

Lola's eyes went dark with distress. "You think the PODS did that?"

"Oh, yeah. They use you up. Then when there's nothing left, they shed you like yesterday's trash." He tried to laugh.

The old guy's hair and beard had grown so long and messy that tiny life-forms had set up home there. He must have been wandering around out here for weeks. Once Miss Rowntree read us a v. depressing poem, *The Ancient Mariner* it was called, about a sailor who stupidly shot an albatross and was doomed to wander the seven seas for ever. I thought maybe he'd looked like this.

Lola had put her hand on Brice's sleeve. "But that didn't happen to you. You got away. Plus you've got friends who really care about you."

They'd obviously forgotten I was there, so I coughed. "At least we know we've come to the right time." I pointed at the old man's shredded sun-faded garments. "Those fastenings are typically Victorian." I knew my fashion, if nothing else.

"Well, if someone doesn't get him out of the sun, this Victorian's a goner," said Brice.

Lola sucked in her breath. "Oh, no, his poor leg!"

The old man's tattered trousers had split at a side seam, exposing a hideous scar around his bony calf.

Brice whistled. "He probably came over to Australia on a transport ship. They used to keep the convicts in leg irons until they got to Botany Bay," he explained.

I stared at him. "A convict? Are you saying he's a criminal?"

"Not necessarily. In his day, just stealing a loaf of bread is enough to get you transported."

"Does it matter, Boo?" said Lola. "He asked us to help."

She's right, I thought. We'd heard his SOS, which made us kind of responsible.

"What can we do, though? We can't exactly move him," I objected.

"We can keep beaming vibes," she suggested.

"If we boost his energy levels, it'll be easier for the Agency to send this guy the help he needs."

We sat down in the desert and beamed vibes until I felt dizzy.

The old man started mumbling to himself. "I put it in my pocket," he blurted suddenly. "I put it in my pocket!"

After half an hour or so, I saw Lola shading her eyes. "Is that a dust devil?"

A huge cloud of dust was travelling towards us. But it wasn't some kind of home-grown Australian whirlwind; it was a wagon pulled by sweating horses.

"Whoa!" The driver jumped down from the wagon and knelt beside the old man. "Wonder how long you've been here, you poor old devil?"

He unstoppered his water bottle and tried to drip some water down the old man's throat, but it ran away into the sand.

"I can't just leave you here," he muttered. The driver was a really sweet guy, also *très* muscly. He lifted the old man easily and laid him in the back of the wagon.

"We'd better go with him," said Lola at once. "To make sure he's OK."

Distances in Australia are really something else.

We went bumping down that track for FIVE hours. Was this really the nearest place the driver could think of? The old man was still raving deliriously about his mysterious pocket.

Poor darling, he's lost it, I thought. I won't pretend I was thrilled at this unexpected diversion, but when you're an angel you have to take the yin with the yang and whatever, and I did feel genuinely sorry for him.

"Yikes, tingles!" squeaked Lola suddenly. "I'm getting major tingles all over."

"Me too," I murmured. "What's doing it?"

"I should imagine it's that rock," said Brice. "Over the rise there."

The glowing red rock formation looked practically extraterrestrial. It was huge, like some massive crouching animal.

"It's out of this world," breathed Lola.

"It is in a way. It's sacred to the Aborigines, so it exists in multi-dimensional reality as well as the three-D kind," Brice told her.

We all gazed at the awesome rock. It was a really special moment. But then Brice had to spoil it. "Oh, the Aborigines are the original Australians, Melanie," he added patronisingly. "The people who don't live here, remember?"

I spent the rest of the journey in huffy silence.

At last we spotted a big plantation of eucalyptus trees. Behind the trees was a wooden church, and beside the church was the mission house, a white-painted building with a large shady verandah.

The driver reined in his team and bellowed a greeting. Two serving women appeared, looking stunned to see another human being.

"Got an old timer in my wagon, half-dead with sunstroke," he told them.

The older woman climbed up and laid her hand on the old man's forehead. "You could fry eggs on him," she muttered.

She frowned as she registered the scars. "You can't bring him in the house," she told the driver. "Convicts make the missus nervous." She gave a rasping laugh. "They made an exception for me. Good cooks are hard to find, eh!"

Luckily the driver was a real charmer and he managed to persuade the women to make up a bed on the verandah. The driver carried the old man into the shade. "I put it in my pocket," the old man moaned. "I put it in my pocket."

"Never mind, grandad," said the woman. "You'll be out of it soon."

"He's had it hard," said the younger woman timidly. "You can see it in his face."

The other servant snorted. "Him? He didn't have to slave in the prison laundry for five years. And he didn't live with a drunken bully and lose two precious little babies to the diphtheria, so don't tell me he's had it hard."

But she wasn't as cynical as she pretended, because with her next breath she told the driver to come round to the kitchen for a feed of boiled mutton and some strong tea. They went into the mission house, leaving the old man alone.

"I can't believe those missionaries won't let a dying man in their house," I said. "I thought Christians were supposed to like, forgive people."

"I'm not convinced he is dying, actually," said Lola. "I'm not getting that death vibe, are you? I don't think he's ready."

I knew what she meant. You could feel the old man's spirit hanging on grimly by its fingernails.

It's almost like something won't let him die, I thought. Like that guy in the albatross poem. A shiver went through me. "Can the PODS do that?" I asked in a panic. "Can they make someone stay alive even if they don't want to?"

"Definitely not," said Brice. "He has to be doing it himself."

*　*　*

Hours passed and still the old man hung on. The fierce heat began to lose its sting and at last the sun went down like a great ball of red fire.

We were watching our human so anxiously that we didn't notice the old Aboriginal woman come out of the bush. She was just suddenly there, padding silently up the wooden steps and on to the verandah. She went straight to the old man, squatted down beside him and started giving him a real telling-off!

As you know, angels understand every human language going, and her scolding went something like this.

"I know why you can't die, you wicked old white fella. You still got work to do. You got a terrible wrong to put right."

It was amazing. The old man instantly calmed down. It was like he actually understood what she was saying. Brice and Lola looked as astonished as I felt.

"That's better," said the old woman. "You been a loud-mouth your whole life. Now listen to someone else for a change. That's good! Now you get to hear the Earth singing to you. You didn't know everything got its own song, even a no-good white fella like you? Well it has." The woman's eyes flickered slyly in our direction. "And these Shining People, they came out of the Dreaming to help me sing it to you."

Omigosh, she must mean us! I thought.

The old woman had begun to chant aloud in her own language.

"Well, show some respect, will you," said Brice impatiently. "She said we'd come to help. So help already!"

That's the amazing thing about the angel business. You never know what's going to happen next. You set off to Victorian London, and before you know it, you're in Australia taking part in a tribal chantathon on a Christian verandah.

But actually it was kind of cool. And after a while this mystical thing happened. I felt the night literally come alive around me. The coolest thing was that I was a part of it. Angels, sacred rocks and eucalyptus trees, mad men and wise old women, we were all a part of the same living, breathing, star-spangled web, and for just a moment we seemed to share one heart and one mind.

Quite suddenly we all stopped chanting and my head filled up with this vast silence. We just sat there without speaking, or even thinking, and it was so peaceful I can't tell you.

The chanting must have been *très* powerful too, because when the sun rose next morning the old man was sleeping like a little baby, and the old woman was nowhere to be seen.

Lola did one of her catlike stretches. "Time to hit the road, guys. Our human's out of the woods. Now it's up to him to sort his life out."

Brice grinned at me. "Are my little Shining People ready to beam themselves to London?"

Beam ourselves! I thought. Omigosh, do we have to?

Brice has this unnerving ability to sense my weaknesses. "Erm, angel tags, sweetheart?" he said sarcastically. "Remember those? You use them to connect with your cosmic power source, blah blah blah."

"I know how angel tags work," I said sniffily. "But what if we end up in the wrong place?"

"Relax, Boo," said Lola. "We've done it before."

Yeah right, from like, a street away, I thought.

Brice's smirk made it clear he thought I was chicken.

"OK, fine!" I said. "Let's beam ourselves to completely the other side of the world. I mean, why worry?" And I grasped my tags and concentrated like crazy.

There are places on Earth where it's almost impossible to get a decent angelic signal, and there are others where the atmosphere is so pure that the connection is instantaneous. The Australian outback is the second kind.

The power surge totally lit up our surroundings, and next minute the glowing desert with its trees and rocks began to stream away from us like flowing lava.

Oh-oh, this is way too mystical for me! Suppose they go and leave me alone in the Dreaming? I panicked. I'll be floating around for ever all by myself.

I was so scared that I just grabbed for Lola's hand and shut my eyes.

To my huge relief, the terrifying cosmic rushing sensation stopped almost as soon as it had begun.

After a few seconds I dared to peek and saw Brice rubbing the feeling back into his fingers.

"You should take up arm-wrestling, sweetheart," he quipped. "You've got quite a grip."

It wasn't Lola I'd clutched in my terror. It was Brice.

CHAPTER THREE

"It seems very different. From Elizabethan times, I mean."

Lola's obvious disappointment penetrated my blur of shame. She hates it, I thought. She thinks I've screwed up big time. And now I came to take in my surroundings, so did I.

We were on a street corner in the East End of London, just before dawn. An old-fashioned gas lamp made a wobbly halo in the fog. Figures toiled past like grey ghosts. They all seemed to be struggling with things that were too heavy for them, lugging baskets or bundles, or patiently dragging home-made carts and trolleys. Soot-blackened tenements loomed over the street, shutting out the sky.

I swallowed. It isn't like this in Sherlock Holmes, I thought.

"Hey, we just went from summer to winter in twenty seconds. That's enough to make anyone feel strange," I said brightly. "The sun will come up in a minute. Then we'll see how cool this is."

Brice pulled his hood over his head. "I wouldn't hold my breath."

A young girl trudged by. "'Oo will buy?" she called in a harsh voice. "'Oo will buy my sweet pippins?"

I saw Brice examining his watch with a baffled expression. It just showed a bizarre row of zeros. So did mine and Lola's.

"Maybe the Dreaming confused them," Lola suggested.

Trainees don't strictly need the Agency's hi-tech watches to monitor the local thought and light levels, or to signal the approach of humans assigned to them. Angels functioned for centuries without the aid of technology and so could we. But the technical hitch made me feel scarily far from home.

Without a word, we set off down the street. Brice was visibly cheesed off, and Lola kept darting him worried looks, like, "Oh, no, poor Brice is in a bad mood."

I scowled to myself. Why did he have to be here? OK, maybe Victorian London wasn't as buzzy and atmospheric as I hoped. But if Lola and I were by ourselves, we'd still be having a laugh. She's not giving it a chance, I thought. She's under this like, sinister Brice spell and she's seeing everything through his eyes.

It wasn't light yet, but all around us Londoners were grimly starting the new day. Shutters went up with a clatter, and sleepy shop assistants came out and started sweeping the pavement, getting ready for business. Since we'd arrived, traffic had been trickling steadily into the city and horse-drawn cabs, carts and omnibuses began to fill the narrow streets.

I noticed Lola peering into a dingy shopfront. Over the door was a painted sign showing three golden balls. The shop window was crammed with old tat: tarnished jewellery, broken clocks, a pair of faded leather gloves worn into holes. Who'd be desperate enough to buy that? I thought.

"What does this shop sell?" Lola asked in a puzzled voice.

"It's a pawnbroker's, sweetheart," Brice told her. "People only come here when they're stony broke. They leave an item as security, a few teaspoons, a necklace or something, and the pawnbroker lends them some cash until they can afford to buy it back. Only mostly they can't, which means the pawnbroker gets to collect."

I quickly moved away. It was the gloves. The thought of anyone wanting to buy them. The thought of anyone being that poor.

I'd pictured Victorian London as scenery basically; a colourful backdrop for a little spot of angelic tourism – the sound of trotting hooves on cobbled streets, hot buttered muffins by the fire. I hadn't thought what it would feel like for humans living there.

A terrifying figure emerged from an alleyway with a bundle of filthy brushes on his back. He was dragging a little boy by the arm. Both man and child were totally black with soot, except for their red-rimmed eyes. The little boy was crying in the hopeless way kids do when they know no-one cares.

"Stop your bleedin' row!" the man yelled. "Or I'll stop it for ya!"

Lola looked shocked. "What's he doing with that little kid?"

"Providing him with a career opportunity," said Brice. "Giving him a chance to be an honest tax-paying citizen."

"That child is tiny. What can he possibly do?"

"He'll fit very snugly inside a chimney," said Brice. "Especially if that nice gentleman gives him a good kicking to help him on his way. Everyone has coal fires these days. Haven't you noticed the soot everywhere? And if you don't sweep your chimneys regularly, darlin', they catches on fire, don't they?"

Lola stared at me. "Boo, tell me he's joking?"

Unfortunately I had to tell her the truth. "He's not. They really do put little boys up chimneys. It's in *Oliver Twist*."

"And this is like, legal?" My mate's eyes were dark with distress.

"You bet," said Brice. "Since the Industrial Revolution, kids are a vital part of the economy. They work as fluff pickers and mud larks and—"

He's doing this on purpose, I thought miserably. He's brainwashing Lola, making her think coming here was a mistake.

It was so unfair. Brice was supposed to look bad, not me.

By this time crowds of office clerks were hurrying through the streets. They were on their way to work, but in their gloomy suits and high stiff collars, they looked more as if they were going to a funeral.

Brice was still reeling off facts.

"Most of these sad characters work in the counting houses in the city," he said. "What a way to spend your life, copying figures into ledgers all day."

But I didn't need an ex-PODS agent to tell me how hard these people's lives were. I could see it in their bleak expressions and their unhealthy complexions, as if they rarely saw daylight.

It's like they're trapped in some nightmare machine and don't know how to get off, I thought. I was feeling fairly trapped myself.

Lola gave me a searching look. "Did you do that protection thingy?" she murmured. "Because you look a bit rough."

Oh, no wonder! I thought. What with my little hand-holding humiliation earlier, and the watches malfunctioning, I'd forgotten to do my usual landing procedure. Which meant that basically since I got here, I'd been soaking up negative vibes like a sponge.

I mentally instructed my angelic system to protect itself from any cosmic toxins in the locality.

"Shouldn't we be running into our human at some point?" I said aloud.

"You'd think," said Lola.

A horse-drawn cab pulled up to the curb. A middle-aged lady got out carrying two carpet bags.

The street was really busy by this time, so she started off towards the crossing. I don't know if it was her crinoline or the corset underneath that made her take such little steps, but it made her look like she was on tiny wheels! When she reached the crossing, I saw the lady crinkle her nose. There were piles of horse manure everywhere.

Suddenly a little boy appeared, flourishing a bald-looking broom. He made a bow to the lady and grandly swept all the poo out of her path.

The lady fumbled in her purse and gave him a very small coin.

"I'll carry them bags for yer, if you like, lady!" he said eagerly. "I'll carry them to Timbuctoo if you just says the word."

She clutched her bags. "Certainly not! Such impudence! Run along, you little guttersnipe. Shoo!"

"Stop thief!" An older boy came haring across the street complaining at the top of his voice. "Turned me back for a second and the little tea-leaf swiped me broom!" he panted.

"Call that a broom?" jeered the little urchin. "Where I come from, we calls that a stick." He flung down the broom and legged it down the nearest alleyway.

For no obvious reason we all went chasing after him.

The people in the tenements had strung their washing across the alley. Victorian pantaloons, nightgowns and petticoats hung limply overhead in the stagnant London air.

In mid-sprint, Lola and I exchanged glances.

"It's him, isn't it?" I panted. "He's our kid?"

I saw Brice grinning to himself.

"What's so funny?"

"Nothing," he smirked.

"Can you believe that!" said Lola breathlessly. "We went all the way to Australia and we still hooked up with our human!"

"Agency timing is quite cool," Brice admitted.

"What about PODS timing?" The remark slipped out before I thought.

"Also excellent," he said coldly.

Lola gave me a look. Like, how could you be so mean? So I gave her a look right back. Like, was I being mean?

Our human slowed down to a leisurely amble, but you could see he didn't totally relax. He was like an animal in the wild, noticing the smallest sound or movement, alert for trouble.

They've picked us a real character this time, I thought.

He wore a battered stove-pipe hat and a

swallow-tail coat at least two sizes too big for him. The coat was full of holes which he'd tried to mend with jazzy remnants, including a bit of old curtain. But he had this air of genuine dignity, as if his hand-me-downs were just a costume he was wearing for the time being.

We trailed our little urchin through a maze of sleazy courts and alleyways and finally emerged in a street market.

It was completely mad. Stall holders competing for who could yell the loudest. Two women having a cat fight, literally pulling out clumps of hair! Plus a driver was backing a brewery wagon into a very narrow entry, while bystanders yelled contradictory advice.

But the little boy in the patchwork coat just sauntered through the mayhem, dodging all the slippery cabbage leaves and fruit peel underfoot, and cheerfully scuffing up dirty hay with his boots as if it were autumn leaves. He was having his breakfast on the move, helping himself to a bread roll when the baker's boy wasn't looking, sneaking a quick dipper of milk from under the milkman's nose.

He strolled up to a stall selling the lurid Victorian horror comics known as Penny Dreadfuls and started reading furtively, while he munched away on a stolen apple.

Eek, I should be taking notes, I thought, and I fumbled in my bag until I found my notebook.

Our human is probably about ten years old, I scribbled. *But v. undernourished, so looks younger. He can read though he doesn't seem to go to school.*

The comic stall was next to a stand serving freshly-made coffee and cooked breakfasts. An elegantly dressed gentleman stood apart from the regular customers, self-consciously turning his coffee cup in gloved hands, looking as if he'd been up all night.

"Slumming," said Brice knowingly. "You get a lot of that here. Toffs coming down to get their thrills."

"Toffs!" I mimicked. "Who are you? The Artful Dodger?"

I'd become vaguely aware of a news vendor bawling on the other side of the market. I don't know why I suddenly felt so sick. I couldn't even hear what he was saying at first. It was just another raised voice, competing with the voices of barrow boys and costermongers yelling about fresh fish and shallots. And even when I managed to make them out, the words still didn't really register.

"Another murder in Whitechapel. Read all about it!"

I saw people gasp and turn to each other to make sure they'd heard correctly.

"Omigosh," I said. "The Whitechapel Murderer! That's what Victorians called Jack the Ripper."

Lola's face went white. "The Ripper was in these times? Why didn't anyone tell me?"

Brice sounded stunned. "I assumed you knew. That's why I—"

And suddenly I felt as if I was falling through space.

I had actually chosen to come here. I'd even imagined it would be fun, like when my mates and I used to watch dross like *Jeepers Creepers* to scare ourselves into hysterics. But it wasn't thrilling to be on Jack the Ripper's turf for real. It felt unbelievably sordid and scary.

And suddenly I knew what was wrong. It wasn't the fog and soot that made Victorian London so dark and brooding. It wasn't even the poverty. Plenty of times are poor and dirty, but only a small handful are a breeding ground for cosmic evil. And for shallow and pathetic reasons which I was totally ashamed to remember, I had brought my lovely soul-mate to one of them.

CHAPTER FOUR

I'm not going to try to justify what I did next.

OK, so maybe my angelic system was affected by its brief exposure to those negative Victorian vibes. Maybe that clouded my professional judgement. But that's no excuse.

I should have called the trip off then and there. I was going to, I was, honestly. I opened my mouth, drew a big breath – and did absolutely nothing. I pictured Brice smirking to himself as I mumbled my way through my apology, then I pictured Lola and him exchanging glances over my head, and I couldn't do it. I just couldn't give him that kind of satisfaction. There was this crucial split second when I could have, *should* have, done the right thing and I fluffed it. What can I say?

I promised to tell you the whole truth and here it is. Uncut, unvarnished and as you see, deeply unflattering to yours truly.

"He's on the move again," hissed Lola.

Our human was making for a stall, where a woman in a filthy bonnet had various hot suet puddings for sale. "Well, it's my little Georgie," she said. "'Ow's tricks?"

I was still inwardly freaking at what I'd done, but I couldn't bear to think about it, so I whipped out my notebook and scribbled frantically, *Our human's name is Georgie.*

Georgie produced a coin from an inside pocket. "I'll have a ha'porth of the plum," he shivered. "But I want it hot, mind."

"I don't blame you, dear! Perishin' today, ain't it?" The pudding lady gave him a toothless grin. "I'll tell you what I'll do. You run and fetch me a drop of what does your 'eart good!" She gave him a conspiratorial wink. "And I'll give you a bit of plum duff for nuffin'."

"Is that code?" whispered Lola.

Brice grinned. "She's sending him to buy gin. Gin is the poor man's tipple," he explained. "Life doesn't seem quite so bad when you see it through a boozy blur."

The gin shop was in the most depressing street I have ever seen. The houses were all on the verge of falling down. People had stuffed old rags and newspapers into the cracks in an attempt to keep out the cold. I couldn't believe anyone really lived here, but if you listened you could hear them clattering cooking pots and soothing crying babies inside.

In these surroundings, the gin shop, with its fancy sign and plate-glass windows, stood out like a palace. Inside everything was bright and gleaming: the polished mahogany of the bar, the brass rails, the giant gin casks painted glossy green and gold. The barrels were labelled with enticing names, like Real Knock-me-down, and Celebrated Butter Gin.

It seemed early to be knocking back the hard stuff, but some of the customers already smelled of drink. One half-starved woman was shushing a toddler.

"Never mind, dearie," cackled an old lady. "A few drops of gin in 'is bottle and 'e'll sleep good as gold."

Georgie bought something called Regular Flare-up. As soon as he was outside the shop, he took a furtive swig. He shuddered, wiped his mouth then raced back to claim his free plum duff.

I was starting to feel as if I was trapped in the opening scenes of *Oliver!*. Georgie ran about the streets for hours, running errands, taking messages, carrying parcels for toffs.

Wherever we went, Londoners were talking about the Whitechapel murders. I began to know when people were going to bring it up. They all had this same expression on their faces, a scared, sick fascination. They were Jack the Ripper addicts, swapping the latest lurid rumour, endlessly rehashing horrific details. It's like they couldn't stop talking about it.

Georgie stood in the barber's for ages, waiting to deliver one of his messages. He kept clearing his throat, waiting for someone to notice him, but everyone was too busy speculating about the Ripper's true identity.

Someone's cousin had seen a suspicious figure with a doctor's bag, fleeing the murder scene. Others had heard of a foreigner with a gold-topped cane in which he concealed his deadly weapon. One customer swore it was the killer's perfume that marked him out. "Sweet, like lily of the valley. It's to cover the smell of the blood," he explained with relish. "It's that scent what'll give him away, mark my words."

"Nuffin' won't give 'im away," the barber chipped in. "Our Jack's too clever for 'em."

"I heard that Scotland Yard know who it is," said his customer through a froth of shaving foam. "I heard, they'd been asked to hush it up."

The barber stopped with the razor in his hand. "Why would they do a thing like that?"

"It's obvious, isn't it? It's got to be a member of the Royal Family."

In the street outside, some guy was buttonholing anyone who'd listen. "It's a Hebrew conspiracy!" he shouted, spraying spit. "Send them murdering Jews back where they come from. Coming here, taking food out of our children's mouths!"

I think that was too much for Georgie. Without any warning he bolted into a side street. Outside a tumbledown tenement, two kids, brother and sister, were crouching in the gutter. They looked blue with cold. Drunken shouts drifted from an upstairs window.

Yet only five minutes' walk away everything was peaceful. I could hear a little winter bird tweeting, and the sound of someone busily scrubbing something with a brush.

Georgie turned into somewhere called Milkwell Yard. The houses were small and narrow but well cared for. Outside Number 7, a maid was polishing a brass knocker.

"Hello, Ivy," said Georgie.

She beamed at him. "Why it's Georgie Porgie! Haven't seen you for days. Too busy kissing the girls, I suppose!"

"You suppose wrong," he said cheerfully. "I've got business to attend to."

Ivy laughed. "'Ark at you! You sound just like a gent on the Stock Exchange! Go round the back, lovie, but keep your voice down. The mistress had another bad night." She gave him a grin. "If you ask me, the spirits are getting their revenge!"

I assumed this was another reference to gin, but then I saw the name on the brass plate. *Miss Minerva Temple, Medium.*

I nudged Lollie. "Is that cool or what!"

She looked uneasy. "Doesn't that mean she talks to the dead?"

"Yeah, Victorians were really into it. We are going to get so many brownie points for this. Mr Allbright is going to love us for ever!"

We followed Georgie down some steps.

A fair-haired girl rushed to open the door.

"Georgie! Where have you been? I was worried something had happened to you."

Georgie's sister was so pale, you could see daylight through her, except for her cheeks which were bright pink. In her lavender gown and button boots, she looked like a little china doll.

She dropped her voice. "We'll have to be quiet," she whispered. "Miss Temple is feeling fragile this morning."

"She still treats you well I hope, Charlotte?"

Hello! I thought. Georgie had completely changed his way of talking. He sounded almost posh.

"Oh, no, she is really kind," his sister reassured him. "She's extremely satisfied with my work. She says my face is wonderfully ethereal!" Charlotte's giggles turned into a long coughing fit.

"I'm afraid you are getting ill, Charlie," said Georgie anxiously.

She shook her head. "Don't be silly! I just catch my breath sometimes."

As the children chatted, I noted down useful facts for Mr Allbright. Georgie and Charlotte were orphans. Their mother had died only a couple of years ago. Until recently, both kids were surviving on the streets, by selling matches and bootlaces. It was

Georgie who had found his sister her unusual post as a medium's assistant. Georgie was the youngest, yet he was fiercely protective of his sister, wanting to know if Miss Temple was working her too hard.

Charlotte said the hardest part was trying not to laugh when Miss Temple pretended the spirit guides were speaking through her. "She sounds exactly like a bullfrog!" She broke off to cough, and this time she couldn't seem to stop. It sounded like rusty machinery rattling inside her.

"The poor kid's got TB," Brice said in a low voice.

"Don't be stupid!" I hissed. "Charlotte's fine. Look at her pink rosy cheeks."

"That's what TB looks like in the early stages," he said grimly. "Until they start coughing blood."

I forced myself to count to ten. I knew what he was up to. He wanted to make me look bad in front of Lola.

"Victorians didn't all have TB," I muttered.

Brice heard. "No, some of them died of diphtheria and typhus and cholera. Also polio and scarlet fever and pernicious anaemia—"

"Give it a rest!"

"Boo, chill out! Brice knows what he's talking about."

Yeah, but why did he have to keep ramming it down my throat?

Georgie fetched his sister a glass of water and she gulped it down. He sat down beside her and they leaned their foreheads together like two babes in the wood.

"Your cough's not getting any better," Georgie said in a worried voice. "I'm going to see our uncle."

Charlotte looked panic-stricken. "Georgie, don't, not after last time."

"I'm going. I don't care," he said. "We've got to get you to a doctor."

She threw her arms round his neck. "Oh, Georgie, I wish we had someone to turn to!"

"We have, stupid, we've got Uncle Noel," he said stiffly. "It wasn't him who tried to have us sent to the workhouse. He was horrified when he heard what Aunt Agnes had been up to. He's a good man, Charlotte, and he has suffered a great deal."

"Has he?" said Charlotte doubtfully. "He seems fortunate to me. He is a very successful lawyer, and they have that fine house."

"He has done very well for himself," Georgie agreed. "But it must have been terrible when he was growing up, having to pretend his mama was a respectable widow, when she wasn't even married. Then Grandfather refused to acknowledge him as his son and heir. My uncle had nothing but bad treatment from our family, Charlie, yet he feels responsible for us. He said he would have us to live with him at Portman Square, if Aunt Agnes wasn't such a witch."

His sister laughed. "He didn't call her a witch!"

"No, she's more like his gaoler!" said Georgie. "He can't spend a farthing without having to account to her. It must torture him seeing us living from hand to mouth, when he has the means to help us. I'm sure that's why he sends me on these strange errands to Newgate. It's just an excuse to give me a few pence."

"How *is* Mr Godbolt?" said Charlotte.

"He seemed frail last time I was there, but then he must be quite old by now."

"Did our uncle ever tell you what Mr Godbolt did to get put in prison?" Charlotte asked.

"He just says, 'Edwin Godbolt made one fatal mistake. But he was a faithful employee for many years and though the law has found him guilty, I will not abandon him.' You see what a fine man he is, Charlie?"

A clock began to strike somewhere in the house. Charlotte jumped up. "I must go! Miss Temple is holding a seance in a few minutes."

"This we have to see," I said to Lola.

She looked uneasy. "I don't know if I want to see a woman pretending to talk to the dead."

"Oh, come on, babe, it'll be *très* educational!"

Her lips curved into a wicked smile. "OK," she agreed. "So long as we don't have fun."

We left Georgie drinking cocoa with Ivy and followed Charlotte into the back parlour. She immediately started peering under tables and into light fittings.

"Yikes!" I said. "This house needs some serious Feng Shui!"

"What's Feng Shui?" Lola said.

"It's basically Chinese for chucking out your clutter," I explained.

I have never seen so much stuff in one tiny room. I don't know how Charlotte managed to move around without knocking anything over.

Like, the table was covered with a fringy chenille cloth. The sideboard had lacy doodads on it, and there was a bigger lacy doodad draped over the back of an armchair. There was a bowl of artificial fruit under a glass dome, plus there were real ferns inside a big glass bottle. And I haven't even got round to the footstools or the embroidered fire screen, ornamental photograph frames or the potted aspidistras!

Having checked that her spirit FX equipment was in working order, Charlotte dragged the heavy curtains across the window, plunging the parlour into artificial twilight. A few minutes later Ivy showed a middle-aged couple into the parlour. I noticed that Charlotte greeted them in a hushed tone quite unlike her normal voice. "Mr and Mrs Bennet, please take a seat. Miss Temple will be with you shortly."

"Hope she doesn't cough," Brice said under his breath. "A coughing medium's assistant wouldn't be nearly so ethereal."

I'd expected Minerva Temple to be got up like a fortune teller with tinkly beads, but when she came in she was dressed really tastefully in a plain black gown and a pretty lace cap trimmed with ribbons. Her voice was low and thrilling. In fact she'd have made an excellent stage hypnotist, which she kind of was in a way.

Minerva set about lulling her victims into a receptive state, reassuring the couple that their daughter was now happy in the fields of Eternal Summer. Mrs Bennet gasped but her husband just fiddled with his collar, looking really uncomfortable.

Everyone held hands around the table and Minerva went into a trance. At least she did some bizarre writing and heavy breathing, which apparently meant the spirits were trying to get through.

Minerva had obviously coached Charlotte to produce 'psychic phenomena' on cue. So when her employer cried, "The veil between the worlds is growing thin!" Georgie's sister pulled a secret handle, releasing a blast of cold air from the cellar, to give the impression that spirits had wafted in from the other world.

Of course, typical Melanie – when I suggested gatecrashing these people's seance, I hadn't actually thought it through. I just wanted to tell my mates I'd been to a bona fide Victorian seance. But I began to feel terribly sorry for those grieving parents. The woman was clearly desperate for reassurance that her daughter still survived, even if it was on the wrong side of the 'veil', and I think the husband only came because of his wife.

The worst moment was when this like, radioactive green stuff started oozing out of Minerva. It flowed out of her mouth and nose, even her ears, and collected in a glowing green puddle on the table.

The husband instantly reached out to touch it.

"Don't!" Charlotte said in a warning voice. "Ectoplasm is harmful to the living. The spirits send it only to reassure you of their existence."

"It's actually cheesecloth and luminous paint," Brice told us in a stage whisper. "She'll make it disappear again in a sec. That way no-one can examine it too closely."

I was still in shock from the ectoplasm when I realised we were not alone. I'm serious – some real ghosts had turned up to Minerva's seance!! They were kind of sepia-coloured and flickery, like figures in old movies. A few of the livelier spirits hovered over the table. The rest just hung around in the background looking depressed.

I gave them a little wave. "Oh, hiya!" Then, "How come they're here?" I hissed to Brice.

"Who did you expect to come to a seance?" he muttered. "Living people?"

It's not just embarrassing watching someone conduct a phony seance with disapproving real-life spirits looking on, it's totally excruciating. Also Mr Bennet was looking increasingly fidgety. Eventually he couldn't contain himself, and cut right across Minerva's gushy portrait of their daughter's lovely personality. "You could be describing any young girl!" he objected.

Minerva's otherworldly expression made it clear she was above such petty remarks, but after a while she began to jerk around in her chair going,

"The spirits are saying there's a doubter in our midst."

Under cover of darkness, Charlotte activated another device, and the table started to jump around as though the spirits were having a tantrum. The real spirits looked more depressed than ever.

Brice hooted with laughter. "Oh rock'n'roll! This woman is outrageous."

I thought I saw Minerva's eyelids quiver then, but next minute she was going on about someone with the initial A, so I decided I'd imagined it.

I think everyone was relieved when that seance was over, including the spirits. Charlotte hurried back to her brother and they talked for a while. Then Georgie said he had to go.

"You will remember to come tomorrow?" Charlotte said anxiously.

Georgie's face suddenly went all pinched. "You needn't keep on. I said I would, didn't I?"

It was the first time he'd sounded like a whingey little kid, and I wondered what had upset him.

Outside, veils of yellowish-green fog swirled through the dusk, reminding me unpleasantly of ectoplasm.

Lola sighed. "I felt so sorry for that Mrs Bennet."

"I kept thinking of my mum. I hate to think what a medium would say about me," I said gloomily.

Lollie squeezed my hand. "She'd say, 'I've got this cute hip hop chick here in a vintage top and she wants you to know she's totally totally fine'!"

I felt a rush of affection for my lovely friend.

I wanted to tell her how I was kicking myself for insisting on coming to a time that was mainly notorious for a pervy killer. But most of all I wanted to say how crazy it felt to be missing her like this, when she was actually right here beside me.

Unfortunately, Brice was there too, mooching along with his hands in his pockets, so I swallowed down my feelings and the words went unsaid.

CHAPTER FIVE

The rattle of late-night sewing machines came from an upstairs sweatshop just off Brick Lane. It was eight o'clock in the evening, but for these Londoners, the working day still wasn't over.

Georgie had run his final errand of the day, rushing two hot kidney pies (euw!) to a reasonably famous Victorian comedian called Dan Leno. Mr Leno was doing a gig at one of the music halls in Curtain Road. We actually caught some of his act.

Then we hitched a lift in a brewery wagon and now we were walking along in the gaslight, enjoying the scene. The streets were crowded with Cockneys out to have a good time. For once, the atmosphere was really mellow. In some streets people had set up shooting galleries and sideshows. There was a guy selling something advertised as 'Wizard Oil' and I could hear a voice bawling, "Step right in and see Hercules, the world's strongest man!"

Further down the street were booths advertising unusual sights for people to marvel at, like 'A Genuine Mermaid', and 'The Dog with Lion's Claws'. But I wasn't seriously tempted, until I saw the big queue forming outside the peepshow. I'd heard about these Victorian entertainments, where you paid your penny to see a magic, or maybe a v. saucy scene.

The party mood was infectious, so I decided to take a look.

To my annoyance Brice yanked me out of the queue. "Where do you think you're going?"

"Well, duh! Obviously I want to see the peepshow."

"Trust me, you don't," he said firmly.

When Brice explained that people were queuing to see waxworks depicting the Ripper's crimes, I felt sick to my stomach. "Little kids are in that queue," I said in horror. "Mums with *babies*."

But Georgie quickened his pace just about then so we had to go hurtling after him. The bustle and noise faded behind us, and we were in the back streets of Whitechapel where street lights were few and far between. Lollie and I had already agreed that Victorian gaslights were just a leetle bit too atmospheric. They made this creepy hissing sound, plus they cast disturbing shadows, which made every harmless passer-by look like a leering assassin. But it was the areas of total darkness that really gave me the chills.

When I saw the poster in the pub doorway, I looked away as soon as I'd read the part about Scotland Yard offering £100 reward. I knew it must be for anyone who would lead them to the killer. I just didn't want to see it in black and white, not now we were on the Ripper's home territory.

I wondered how Georgie dared to walk these streets alone. It wasn't just the dark and the fog and the creepy gas lamps; it was something in the air, a lurking menace you could almost taste. I was quite glad of Brice slouching beside us, doing his 'don't mess with me' walk.

In a little lane off Gower's Walk, several heavily made-up girls hung about under a street lamp, shivering in their scanty clothes.

Respectable Victorian women hid their bodies totally from view. What with the corsets and petticoats underneath and the bustles on top, you almost forgot they had normal bodies.

But let me tell you, the Gower's Walk girls were a different species. One was literally spilling out of her blouse, and each time a potential punter came by, they'd all give him a naughty flash of silk stocking. "Take me 'ome with you, mister," one girl called. "I'll show you a good time."

Lola looked distressed. "She's just a kid," she said. "She can't be more than fourteen."

"It's all perfectly legal," Brice told her. "Victorian girls can marry at that age."

"It might be perfectly legal, but it's also perfectly sick," said Lola.

"Well, my stars! Look who the cat brought in!" said a husky voice.

A girl with rouged cheeks and a pink feather boa was grinning unmistakably at Brice.

No way! I thought. NO way!

It's not that I'm a prude. It had just never occurred to me that an Earth angel might hang out with, you know, tarts. Which might be why I'd failed to register the cosmic tingles that let us know when other Light Workers are in the area. Stranger still, this particular angel and Brice were old acquaintances.

"Well, you look in better shape than what you did last time you was here, darlin'," she said. "Go on, introduce me to your pretty girlfriends!"

It was the first time I'd seen Brice blush. "This is Ella," he told us awkwardly. "Ella, meet Mel and Lola."

"Pleased to meet you," she beamed. "I knew this one would come right in the end," she added in a stage whisper. "'E 'ad sumfin' about 'im, know what I mean?"

"So do you work erm, in this lane every night?" Lola asked.

"Someone's got to do it, darlin'. If nuffin' else we can keep the fear levels down."

Ella explained that the dark powers were actively feeding the public's obsession with the Ripper. With the help of the press, they'd turned a sick killer into a bogeyman, a demon almost.

"Sorry, Ella, we've got to go." I'd spotted Georgie's coat-tails disappearing into the dark. Calling hasty goodbyes, we sped down the street, catching up with him outside a huge derelict building.

Georgie climbed on to a sill, stealthily prised up a sash window, squeezed himself through the gap, and landed softly on the other side. I was just about to jump down after him, when a boy stepped out of the darkness, brandishing some kind of weapon.

"Oi! What's your game? These are prime lodgings! If you want to come in, you gotta show me the colour of your tin."

We climbed in after Georgie, wondering what was going on.

"I ain't got any tin," lied Georgie. "But I got this." He delved inside his coat and brought out half a cigar, which someone had thrown down on the street. "Best Havana," he said enticingly. "Same as they smokes in the 'Ouse of Lords."

The boy examined the cigar critically, then fished out some matches and coolly lit up. "Want a pull?" he offered. "It's a good 'un."

"No thanks, I'm giving 'em up." I could see Georgie was trying not to yawn.

His new landlord tossed him an indescribably filthy blanket. "You're kipping in the Royal Suite tonight," he said loftily. "I do 'ope as the tinkling of the chandeliers won't keep you awake."

I was stunned. Not only had this homeless kid got the nerve to take over an abandoned building, he was actually renting out floor space to other waifs and strays. In every room exhausted children huddled under any covering they could find: a coat, a torn curtain, old newspaper. Georgie was lucky to get that blanket.

I pictured Jade, my little sister, in her twenty-first-century bedroom, with its glowstars and Barbies and stuffed toys. Then I imagined her in this stinking hellhole with cockroaches scurrying over her in the dark, and my throat ached. How could Victorian adults let this happen?

Georgie was so tired that he could hardly stand by this time, but he stumbled around until he found a patch of floor out of the draught. Then he wrapped himself in his blanket and fell asleep in seconds.

"I'm going for a walk," Brice said abruptly. Without any explanation he vanished into the night.

I was just going to say, "Ooh, was it something we said?" when we heard whimpering sounds. Lola and I looked at each other. Officially this was a field trip, not a mission, but you can't ignore a frightened kid. So we went tiptoeing through room after horrible room until we found the little girl who was having a bad dream.

She had sores on her face and her hair was all matted. I don't think anyone had washed or brushed it in her life. "Don't 'urt me!" she pleaded in her sleep. "Please don't 'urt me."

Maybe it was her own personal bogeyman the

little girl was dreaming about, but I doubted it. It was like Ella said, a human killer had become an evil demon. By daylight people's fears were just about manageable. But in the hours of darkness, the spirit of the Ripper terrorised London, turning it into a city of nightmares.

Sometimes Lola and I don't need to speak. We just crouched on the bare boards and comforted the little girl with the gentlest vibes we knew. Very gradually her whimpers stopped.

Lola stroked her dirty hair. "Sweet dreams, little one," she whispered. "Only sweet dreams from now on."

We moved among the sleeping children, doing what we could to heal and comfort them. But I knew it wasn't enough. Depression washed over me. Some of these kids were younger than Jade. They needed homes and parents and a good bath. They shouldn't be living like this.

"This universe sucks," I blurted suddenly. "No-one cares about anyone else, not really."

I was shocked at myself actually, but Lola just looked surprised.

"So why are we here then?" she said.

"Because of our stupid pointless pathetic school project."

And because I screwed up, I added silently.

Lola gave me one of her wise smiles. "You don't believe that, babe."

I felt a microscopic prickle of hope. Maybe my friend wasn't mad with me. Maybe I hadn't screwed up. Maybe, just maybe, this could turn out OK?

Oh, get real Mel! I thought despairingly. This is the first time Lollie and I have been on our own since we got here. We wouldn't even be having this conversation if Brice was here. He has to ruin everything.

Then a shameful thought slithered into my mind. Maybe Brice wouldn't come back. Maybe he'd defected to the PODS, once and for all, and vanished from our lives for ever.

CHAPTER SIX

The night sky outside the windows was fading to the colour of grubby smoke. Lola and I were taking a break, sharing a pack of angel trail mix. It was almost like old times. Just being in that rat-infested house with her, munching and scribbling notes for school, not even talking that much, made me ridiculously happy.

Then suddenly Brice was lounging in the doorway with that twisted smile on his face. "How's it going?" Despite the cold he was just wearing jeans and a Bruce Lee T-shirt.

"We're good!" Lola beamed. "As you see, we're stuffing our faces." She rattled the packet. "Want some?"

He shook his head. "No thanks. It feels much better in here, by the way. You two did a great job with the light levels."

"Yeah, thanks for helping. Not!" I scowled. "So where've you been?"

"Oh, you know, checking out the sights."

"In the dark?" I said disbelievingly. "Yeah right."

Lola noticed him shivering. "Babe, what happened to your hoodie?"

Brice shrugged. "Must have left it somewhere."

All around us, kids were surfacing from sleep. The younger children still looked soft-eyed and dreamy. The older ones immediately snapped into survival mode, stowing their pathetic bedding out of sight, stuffing scraps of food into their mouths.

Georgie had been using his coat for a pillow, but when he tried to put it back on, his arm got stuck in the torn lining of his sleeve. He had to rip the lining out to free himself. Perhaps it was because he wasn't totally awake that he looked so sad and bewildered. But as I watched him struggling into his outsized coat, I felt this unbearable pity well up inside me. I couldn't take it, and tried to laugh it off.

"What's up with our little Master Sunshine today?" I asked the others.

"Isn't it obvious?" said Brice. "The kid's life stinks!"

"Presumably it stank yesterday, but he was as lively as anything," I objected.

But as I watched Georgie drearily fastening his buttons, I wondered if this was true. Maybe his cheeky Cockney routine was something he put on to survive, like his badly-fitting clothes.

We followed him back into the street and were instantly engulfed by a billowing snot-green cloud. I've never seen fog like it. This must be what they mean by a Victorian pea-souper, I thought.

"It's been like this for hours," said Brice.

Lollie covered her nose. "It smells rank!"

Victorian London had a really peculiar pong: a mix of bad drains, terrible Victorian cooking and leaking gas, plus the suffocating stink caused by Londoners burning coal twenty-four seven. Unfortunately the dense fog was preventing these toxic smells from escaping into the upper atmosphere.

The Hell dimensions can't smell any worse than this, I thought. The topic of hellish smells naturally led on to thinking about Brice. He could have spent the night plotting with his old PODS cronies and we wouldn't be any the wiser. Well, he'd better not be plotting to hurt me and Lola, or he'd be sorry.

The lonely sound of a foghorn floated out of the murk. I couldn't believe people would take boats and barges out in this weather – the visibility was practically down to zero. If we let Georgie get more than a few inches ahead, he totally vanished from view. We blundered past looming shapes which I guessed to be warehouses and cranes. I'd assumed Georgie was carrying out one of his errands, but as we trudged on and on, I began to suspect he was just walking aimlessly.

We followed him under a dank old bridge and came out opposite a park. After a nervous look round, Georgie nipped through the gates, darted to the nearest flower bed and started picking Michaelmas daisies, which happened to be the only plants in flower. When he had a sizeable bunch, he made a speedy exit.

"What is the boy up to?" Lola said.

"I don't know, but he looks seriously stressed," Brice said.

By the time we'd reached the medium's house in Milkwell Yard, we could see Georgie visibly bracing himself for some major ordeal.

Ivy met him at the back door, with her finger to her lips. "Your sister says she hopes you don't mind waiting," she said in a hoarse whisper. "But a client turned up, total stranger, he was. Just rang the bell, bold as you like. Says his name's Smith." She gave a disbelieving snort. "I said, 'I'm sorry, sir, but Miss Temple won't see you without an appointment, not if you was Prime Minister.' But he comes out with this cock and bull story about his dead granny and how he needs the spirits to help his family find her will."

She leaned closer. "I think he's one of those whatsisname, investigators, trying to catch her out. I said to her, 'Madam, you don't have to see him.' But she says, 'Ivy, my professional reputation is at stake!'"

Ivy noticed Georgie anxiously clutching his daisies and her eyes filled with pity. "Oh, bless," she exclaimed softly. "And here's me rabbiting like it's just an ordinary day."

She suddenly took in his bedraggled appearance. "Tell you what, 'ow'd you like a nice wash, while you're waiting?" she said briskly. "I'll fry you some bacon and eggs and you have a little clean-up, how about that?"

Ivy seemed to know about Georgie's forthcoming ordeal, and was reminding him, in the kindest possible way, that he should make himself look more respectable.

"Let's give the kid his privacy," Brice suggested. "We can have fun with Minerva's paranormal whatsisname while we wait."

Lollie shook her head. "One seance was enough."

"Oh, come on. This one will be a blast," he insisted.

"You're a bit confident, aren't you?" I said.

"I'm totally confident, sweetheart, and I'll tell you why." Brice paused for dramatic effect. "Minerva Temple heard us talking last night!"

We stared at him.

"I'm serious. She has a genuine psychic gift. You saw what happened yesterday. She's a spirit magnet. They can't keep away from her."

"But that doesn't make sense!" I objected. "If she's for real, why go in for fake ectoplasm and funny voices?"

"Because the spirit world is unpredictable, and if you don't give the punters what they want, they won't pay up. Faking it is a safer bet."

"Well, I don't think we should get involved," I said in my prissiest voice. "She's conning vulnerable people. This guy should just go ahead and expose her."

"Maybe you should see what's going on, before you make up your mind," Brice said.

We argued for a bit, but I admit I was a leetle bit curious to see this mysterious Mr Smith myself, so I eventually let myself be persuaded. We crept into the purple twilight of Minerva's parlour. The bored ghosts were killing time playing a game of ghostly noughts and crosses. They didn't have a pencil or paper, so they took it in turns to draw on the mirror with a spooky sepia finger.

Minerva, Georgie's sister and Mr Smith were holding hands in hushed silence, waiting for the fake spirits to show.

After the usual heavy breathing, Minerva announced that Mr Smith's dead grandmother was standing by her side. "She is showing me a beautiful brooch," she said in her hypnotist's voice. "A very old cameo brooch. She tells me she was very fond of it and sometimes used it to fasten her shawl."

Mr Smith shook his head in mock amazement. "What are the chances of anyone guessing that an old lady would wear a shawl and a cameo brooch? Could you ask her if she ever owned a pair of spectacles?"

Brice's instincts were right about this guy. Most paranormal investigators are genuinely after the truth, but this guy wasn't one of them. He didn't just want to expose Minerva and put her out of business. He wanted to destroy her, as a person.

He sat forward and I saw his eyes glitter in the twilight. "Perhaps you could ask my grandmother about someone who used to work in her kitchen? A workhouse girl. I think her first name was Minnie," he mused. "And her last name began with T. It was strangely similar to your own, Miss Temple. Could it be Tuttle? Yes, that's it. Could you ask my dear old granny whatever happened to little Minnie Tuttle?"

Minerva's voice sounded strained. "I don't appear to be getting anyone of that name," she said bravely.

Omigosh, I thought, the poor darling. It's her! *She's* Minnie Tuttle.

This guy had evidently been digging around in her past, a past Minerva found so painful that she'd invented a whole new identity for herself.

"Figured out whose side you're on yet?" Brice whispered.

"Yeah, this creep's got it coming," I agreed. "But what can we do? We're totally not meant to interfere."

He grinned. "And we're not going to." He nodded at the ghosts. 'What do you say, guys? Shall we make it a team effort?"

They looked stunned. One spirit asked Brice something, in a distorted underwatery voice.

"No, seriously," Brice said. "You're the experts. We're just here to help you do your stuff."

It would be completely unprofessional of me to reveal what happened next, so I'll just tell you that ten minutes after we hijacked the seance, the paranormal investigator bolted from the house. The final straw was definitely when Minerva's spirits told her to ask him about an important public examination in which a pupil with the initials O. D. did something he shouldn't.

I know! You have to ask yourself, how do ghosts get hold of this information? How could they possibly know that Mr Smith's real name was Obadiah Dunhill?

I was on such a high that I slapped Brice's palm and said, "Yess!"

"Didn't I tell you it would be a blast?" he boasted.

Lola just beamed at us, like, "You see! These kids can play together nicely if they try."

Minerva was lying back in her chair, sniffing at a bottle of smelling salts. Her spirits hovered solicitously in the background. She looked tired and overwhelmed, but deep down I think she was actually relieved to be back in the bona fide psychic bizz.

Charlotte was pulling back the heavy curtains, letting in what little daylight there was. Then she turned and I saw her face, and my elation died away.

"May I leave now, Miss Temple?" she asked timidly. "You said I could have the morning off? My mama died two years ago today and my brother and I are going to visit her grave."

Lola gave me a helpless look.

So that's why Georgie stole the flowers.

Georgie was waiting in the kitchen, looking astonishingly different without his grime. In fact, he had surprisingly delicate features for a boy. He silently handed half his flowers to Charlotte, and they set off down the street.

Georgie didn't say a word as they walked along. Charlotte kept giving him worried glances, but after ten minutes she couldn't stand it any longer and said, "We must try not to be sad, you know, Georgie. Mama and Papa's troubles are over now. They are with the angels, watching over us from Heaven."

For the first time since we'd met him, Georgie lost his temper. "There IS no Heaven, Charlotte!" he yelled. "The angels didn't help you when you were living on the street. It was me who found you that job. We're on our own. There's just you, me and Uncle Noel, no-one else."

He stormed ahead, leaving a pathetic trail of petals.

Charlotte went hurrying after him. "Wait! Georgie, wait for me!"

"I used to feel like Georgie," Lola murmured. "Didn't you, Mel?"

"Totally," I admitted, "and I didn't have it as hard as these kids."

A fit of violent coughing had stopped Charlotte in her tracks. Georgie ran back looking totally stricken. He waited anxiously until she'd recovered, then he silently took her hand and they walked on together to the church where their mother was buried.

We'd agreed the children should visit the grave on their own, so when we reached the church, we tactfully went off for a walk.

The weather had improved slightly, but left-over fog still clung here and there, wreathing atmospherically around the stone crosses and headstones. Some of the graves had statues of angels watching over them, which Victorians seemed to picture either as big girls with wings, or chubby little cherubs. Lola and I started doing mad angel statue imitations but then a funeral procession came through the gates, so we hastily stopped.

The hearse was a horse-drawn coach, drawn by four black horses in blinkers. Through the window, the polished gleam of the coffin was just visible under heaps of white flowers. A father and his small daughter walked slowly behind, followed by grieving friends and relations. All the women wore long black veils.

Brice was mooching around, examining inscriptions on headstones. I wondered what people would think if they knew a dodgy angel in a Bruce Lee T-shirt was prowling around their graveyard.

The funeral coach went slowly past us, and we all bowed our heads in respect, even Brice. The hollow rumbling of the wheels and the clipping horses' hooves sounded dreamlike and muffled in the fog. One of the horses gave a nervous snort and tossed its ebony plumes.

"I want my mama," the little girl was saying. "Where's my mama?"

I can't handle this, I thought. There's too much death and dying in these times.

I must have looked upset because Lola asked, "Are you OK, hon?" Then I heard her voice change. "Mel, look, there she is!"

A little way off, under the trees, a young woman was watching the funeral. She held a tiny new-born baby in her arms. The mother and baby weren't see-thru and sepia like the spirits in Minerva's parlour. For people who'd so recently died, they looked spectacularly full of life. You could see that dead woman really felt for her husband and daughter, yet her face was filled with utter peace and love.

When will you get it into your head, Melanie? Dying is not the end, I reminded myself. It's not a big hole or a terrifying bottomless pit or a cartoon cliff edge that characters vanish over for ever. It's a portal into a totally limitless, indescribably beautiful universe.

I noticed Brice giving me a funny look, almost but not quite a smile.

"What?" I said. Brice has this annoying habit of spoiling my mystical moments.

"I think the kids are almost finished," he said gruffly.

Georgie and Charlotte had pulled up the weeds growing over their mother's grave. Now they solemnly laid down their flowers. Charlotte said a prayer, stopping once to cough into her handkerchief. Georgie just chewed his lip furiously, but when his sister finished, he muttered "Amen."

The dead woman waved serenely as we left and I waved back.

The children said their goodbyes outside the churchyard. Charlotte wanted her brother to come back to Milkwell Yard, but he said he had something to do. I guessed Georgie planned to drop in on his uncle.

It was a long walk, even with Georgie's impressive knowledge of shortcuts. But I cheered up when I realised Portman Square, where Georgie's uncle lived, joined on to Baker Street. I was walking down the actual street where Sherlock Holmes and Watson hung out solving mysteries! I didn't mention this though. Brice would only try to make me look small.

Sherlock Holmes lived in a flat. I don't think he cared much about worldly goods. Uncovering the truth, that's all he cared about. But Georgie's relations had a big posh house, set behind iron railings.

The maid who opened the door only looked about nine years old. She must have just started working there and obviously didn't recognise Georgie. When she saw him on the step, she clasped her hands behind her back like a child in a talent show.

"The mistress says no hawkers, no traders and no workhouse riffraff," she recited in a pleased voice.

"I'm not selling anything and I'm not riffraff," said Georgie with dignity. "My name is Georgie Hannay. Please tell my uncle I wish to see him, and that it's a matter of life and death."

A few minutes later the maid flounced back, and showed Georgie in to his uncle.

He was sitting by a crackling fire, apparently reading *The Times*. He had long dark hair with dramatic silver streaks. He was actually quite handsome, in a slightly haunted way. A little spaniel was sitting at his feet, longing to be noticed. It gave a joyful bark when we came in and Georgie's uncle looked up.

"Georgie! What is this 'matter of life and death' you have to see me about?"

Georgie stammered out his story. He explained that Charlotte's cough was getting worse and that she urgently needed a doctor. "But we can't afford his fee, so I wondered if you could help us. I promise I'd pay you back," he said anxiously.

The whole time Georgie was talking, his uncle was searching his face with a strangely hungry expression. It wasn't like he was seeing Georgie, so much as looking *through* him to someone else.

"I thought of asking Miss Temple," Georgie babbled nervously. "But if she suspected my sister was ill, she might put her back on the street. I am so afraid Charlotte may have tuberculosis, like mama." His lip trembled.

"You do realise that before I do anything, I must first consult with your aunt, Mrs Scrivener?"

"I understand—" Georgie began.

His uncle cut across him. "I'm afraid you don't. Mrs Scrivener is a formidable woman, some might say frightening, and it is she who holds the purse strings. The fine things you see around us here are mine only through marriage. Your grandfather did not leave me a fortune to squander as he did your dead papa, and if your aunt suspected I was spending her money on my half-brother's brats—"

He saw Georgie go red and added in a gentler voice, "Those are her words, my dear. Your aunt does not feel for you as I do."

Georgie nodded miserably.

"I'm sure this house seems very pleasant, doesn't it?"

"Oh, yes uncle—" Georgie began but his uncle was still talking.

"Well, let me tell you, when Mrs Scrivener has one of her rages, it is a purgatory, a real Dante's Inferno."

"Yes, sir," mumbled Georgie.

Mr Scrivener shook his head, as if he'd just remembered something. "Poor child. How could you have heard of Italy's greatest poet? You don't even go to school. Come, your aunt will not be back for some time. We must have tea before you go."

I've always adored real fires, so I went to warm my hands at the flames. The spaniel immediately came over and lay down beside me. That's one cool thing about being an angel – animals totally worship you.

While they waited for the tea to arrive, Georgie told his uncle about visiting his mama's grave.

His uncle's handsome face flushed. "I believe that your mama's delicate constitution was fatally weakened by that business with your papa."

Georgie looked wistful. "How did Papa die? Mama would never tell us."

His uncle avoided his eyes. "It is better that way," he said. "We must simply pray the weakness has not been passed on to you."

Georgie looked bewildered. "Yes, Uncle."

The tea came and Georgie's uncle plied Georgie with muffins and seed cake and kept refilling his cup with hot sweet tea. The room was very warm, and once Georgie's stomach was full, he had to struggle to stay awake. After a while he began to snore, and his uncle sat watching him with that same strangely hungry expression. I got the feeling Georgie reminded him of someone, someone completely unlike his scary wife.

A new, darker expression came into Georgie's uncle's eyes. He got up abruptly and went to sit at his desk, where he began to compose a letter.

The spaniel couldn't settle with so many angels in one room. It went trotting over to Lola and Brice, wagging its stumpy little tail.

"Nice dog," said Brice softly. "Pity about your psycho master."

The dog gazed at them, as if they were the most wonderful beings it had ever seen. They smiled at each other and their hands touched as they stroked its silky ears.

I was suffering from serious jealousy, I admit that now. But at the time I totally couldn't, so I took my feelings out on Brice. "It's not the uncle's fault he's married to a mean old harpy," I snapped.

"Mel, just ask yourself how two kids from a well-off family came to end up on the streets," Brice said angrily.

"Stuff happens," I said. "You of all people should know that. Anyway, you heard what the uncle said. Georgie's father squandered the family fortune.

Maybe he was a gambler. He obviously had mental problems."

I was horrified at myself. Stop defending this guy, Mel, I thought. You think he's a psycho too.

Brice made a sound of disgust. "That's what Uncle Noel wants people to think. I can't believe you fell for it."

"Even if their dad was a gambler," he said, turning to Lola, "which I doubt, it's likely some of the money was put in trust for them. I have a feeling that nice, caring Uncle Noel used his legal eagle know-how to divert their inheritance to his own personal bank account. Maybe he got himself made executor, so he could 'look after' Georgie and Charlotte's dosh until they come of age. *If they come of age*," he added darkly.

"You mean, Uncle and Auntie Scrivener would prefer it if neither kid survived?" Lola's eyes widened. "Omigosh! Do you think he's psycho enough to kill them?"

"I think he's probably been hoping they'd just die naturally of hunger and neglect. Sounds like the aunt got impatient and tried to have the kids put in the workhouse. Charlotte wouldn't last long in there."

This is so unfair, I thought. I was the Sherlock Holmes fan, not Brice. How come he got to play detective? And how come he and Lola were talking to each other over my head as if I wasn't even in the room?

"Well, I think an angel should always give a person the benefit of the doubt," I said prissily. "Plus you two seem to have forgotten this is only meant to be a field trip. We're not supposed to get involved."

Lollie put her finger to her lips. "Something's happening."

Uncle Noel had finished writing his letter. He slipped it into an envelope, sealing it with hot wax. Then he reached into a money bag hidden at his waist and extracted a shiny silvery sixpenny bit. At last, he went to wake Georgie.

"I want you to take another letter to our old friend in Newgate Gaol. Here is money for a cab and sixpence for yourself. You are to hand this personally to Mr Godbolt. Can you remember my message from last time?"

"I am to tell Mr Godbolt that you have not forgotten about him or his sister," Georgie echoed blearily. He was still half-asleep, but his uncle must have been scared his wife would come back because suddenly Georgie was outside on the doorstep, still struggling into his coat.

He hailed a passing horse-drawn cab and we rode all the way to Newgate Street in unusual style. Georgie was obviously familiar with the drill, and just marched up to the prison door and tugged the bell pull.

I've never seen such an ominous door in my entire existence. The wood was studded all over with iron nails and bound with huge iron bands. The massive bolts were iron too. And this was just the door!

I gulped. We're angels, I reminded myself bravely. We can leave any time we like.

I heard heavy footsteps and the jangling of keys. It was a horribly claustrophobic sound which totally explained why Victorian prison warders used to be known as 'turnkeys'.

A grating slid open. "State your business," growled a voice.

"I'm to take a letter to Mr Edwin Godbolt," said Georgie.

"'I'll see as he gets it."

"It's from 'is brief," said Georgie in his street voice. "I'm to put it in 'is 'and, or I don't get paid."

The bolts rasped back, and a weary looking turnkey let us in to a grim stone hallway. The only source of light came from the glimmering oil lantern in his hand. He was just a tired bloke in a black suit and broad-brimmed hat, but you could see that having those keys made him feel seriously in charge.

The turnkey led us down steps and along twisty passages and through a series of yards, each one guarded by gates with iron gratings. We had to stop at each one, while he put down his lantern, hunted for the right key, unlocked and then relocked the gate after us. The further we went into the prison, the more stale and smelly the air became, as if all the gaol's actual oxygen had been used up years ago.

We came to an immense dank stone room, a cellar basically, with dripping sounds and slimy stuff growing on the walls. The smell was so gross I had to hold my breath. Unbelievably, there was just one toilet bucket for twenty or more convicts to use. Some convicts were trying to sleep on thin mats on the floor. The rest paced or leaned blankly against the walls. One made coaxing noises to Georgie, as if he was a cute little pet. "Come over here, laddie." He leered at the little boy, exposing broken teeth, and Georgie backed away.

The turnkey held up his lamp. "Message for Edwin Godbolt from 'is brief," he said in a bored voice.

An elderly man moved forward into the light. He was pale and painfully thin, but he had the sweetest expression I've ever seen on a human adult. "Georgie, how kind of you to visit me in this fearful place."

"My uncle sent me. He has written you a letter, sir," Georgie explained.

I saw a flicker of emotion in the old man's eyes. "Oh, yes, I should have realised," he sighed. "I haven't received one of those for some time. Thank you, child." Mr Godbolt quickly slipped the envelope inside his thin shirt.

"Don't you want to read it?" asked Georgie in surprise.

The old man smiled. "I have all the time in the world to study its contents. But you are here in person, you precious child, and it does me good to see your face."

"'E looks a bit young to be a solicitor though," someone shouted.

Georgie grinned. "It's my uncle who is a lawyer, not me!"

"No offence to your uncle, nipper, but 'e can't be up to much," said the same joker, "or this old darlin' wouldn't be languishing here along with all us villains. I've been banged up with real forgers, right? And this one don't have the look, know what I mean?"

"'E's like our dear old Granddad, Mr Godbolt is," said a young inmate unexpectedly.

"Yes, yes, he's a regular Saint Francis," said the turnkey gruffly, "and all the mice do little tricks for him on Sundays. Have you finished your business, lad? I've got a nice lamb chop going cold in my office."

"No, sorry," said Georgie. "Mr Godbolt, my uncle says I am to tell you that he has not forgotten about you or your sister." He smiled at the old man, clearly proud of his uncle's generosity.

The old man closed his eyes and took a breath, and when he opened them his voice was almost completely steady. "Thank you very much, child. Take care of yourself, won't you, until we meet again."

It should have been a relief to hit the streets, but no matter how fast I walked I couldn't shake off that icky prison vibe.

No-one in this city is free, I thought miserably. Victorian London is just one big fogbound prison. Normally I'd have squeezed Lola's hand for comfort, but Brice was in between us. So we just kept walking in grim silence until we'd walked all the way back to Whitechapel.

Then I heard Brice say, "I can understand you being upset. Newgate kills me every time." And the creep put his arm through Lola's.

I'd had about enough of being invisible, so I grabbed Lola's other arm and started wittering about how the fog was making my hair frizz.

With a swift movement, Lola pulled herself free. "Stop this, both of you!" she blazed. "You haven't even noticed that Georgie's upset!"

At that moment I couldn't have cared less about him. I was totally not in angelic mode. Lollie had just yelled at me, ME, her best friend! Plus she'd bracketed me unforgivably with Brice.

I glowered resentfully at Georgie. He was standing absolutely still under a street lamp, clutching a silver locket and peering at it in the flickery light with a weirdly intense expression. I'm ashamed to say I assumed that he'd stolen it from his uncle, because of Charlotte. Then I noticed that Georgie had his back to an alleyway, and I thought, this kid's too savvy to check out stolen goods in public. And then I saw a tear tracking down his face, and I thought Lola's right. I never even noticed.

The little boy shut his eyes and pressed the cold silver to his lips. That's when I knew for sure that the locket must be his. His hand shook slightly as he opened the locket, and when he saw the picture inside, a sob burst out of him.

"I'm trying to be strong, Mama," he whispered. "I try, but I get so scared."

At that moment someone came out of the alley and went hurrying past. For an instant I saw a blurred figure, sharply outlined in the gaslight. Then it melted back into the darkness.

Afterwards, the others asked me to describe what I'd seen. Had I seen a surgeon's bag, or an exotic gold-topped cane, that might have concealed the lethal knife? Did I notice an overpowering scent of lily of the valley? But all I could remember was the shadow of a hat and cloak flowing along the wall, monstrous and distorted in the gaslight, and the sensation of something soft and velvety brushing against my energy field. I pulled back. I remember that, but it was pure instinct. I wasn't consciously paying attention to the stranger in the cloak. I was angry with myself because Lola was right about me, plus I was angry with *her* for exactly the same reason.

I put my hand to my face. Something was wrong.

Something had disturbed my energy field so badly that I thought I might actually faint.

"Lola," I began. "I need to sit d—"

Bloodcurdling screams came from the darkness. A girl shrieked, "Get the police!"

Scared faces appeared at windows all along the street.

Someone blew several blasts on a whistle and I heard the pounding of feet as Victorian bobbies ran to the scene. There was a babble of voices, inarticulate with horror.

"Omigosh, Georgie!" said Lola. "Mel, Brice, quick!"

Georgie's face was deathly pale in the gaslight. "He walked past me," he whispered. "Jack the Ripper just walked right past me."

CHAPTER SEVEN

When a defenceless kid has just bumped into Jack the Ripper, the question of breaking cosmic rules doesn't really apply.

"There's a pub down the road, you can see it from here, The Three Cripples," said Brice. "It's basically a dive but the landlady's sound. She'd probably let Georgie stay the night."

We clustered round the traumatised Georgie, and told him firmly and clearly to get himself to Brice's dodgy pub right away.

"You need to be where there are lights and people, kiddo," said Brice.

I felt a zing of angel electricity inside my heart as Georgie got the message. He looked wildly up and down the street and I could hear him thinking, "Lights, people!" He spotted a faint gleam from the pub across the street, and set off at a trot. I heard him repeating Brice's words out loud. "I've got to be where there are lights and people."

The pub door stood slightly open, leaking smells of mice and old beer and stale cooking. Inside a man with multiple tattoos was telling some equally scary men about the latest killing.

Georgie slid around the customers, edging as close to the fire as he dared. He was shivering uncontrollably by this time. A bald-looking dog came to sniff at his hands. "Good dog," Georgie said shakily. "Who's a good dog."

"Are you all right, nipper?" called the tattooed guy. "You looks a bit green around the gills."

A tremor ran through Georgie. "I seen Jack," he said in his street voice. "But I never knew I seen 'im, if you know what I mean. That's why I come here where there was lights and people. I couldn't stand it out there alone in the dark." Georgie buried his face in his hands, and the ugly dog tried to lick him through his fingers.

The landlady had heard Georgie's distraught explanation.

"You stay where you are, littl'un," she said. "As it happens I've got some victuals need eating up, and, well, if you happens to fall asleep by the fire, I'm so rushed off me feet, I probably won't notice till morning."

Lola gave a sigh of gratitude. "You're right, she's a total sweetie. It's so great you knew about this place, Brice."

"Yeah, well, any time you need a criminal hangout, just ask Brice," I said sarcastically.

I could see Lola inwardly counting to ten. "That's not what I mean Boo, and you know it."

"So why do you reckon Uncle Noel is blackmailing Mr Godbolt, Lollie?" Brice asked her over my head.

"Hello!" I said. "You have absolutely no evidence for that accusation. For all you know, Georgie's uncle genuinely wants the guy to know he hasn't abandoned him, even though he's a convicted criminal."

"Hello!" Brice mimicked. "That message about the sister sounded like a nasty little threat to me."

"Not everyone is a nasty little double-crosser, you know, hint hint," I told him.

Lola shook her head. "There's no need to be mean. And actually I agree with Brice."

"Oh there's a surprise!" I was practically spitting with rage.

"I'm just telling you what I think, Boo! Georgie's uncle knows something he's not saying. And that sweet old guy in the prison KNOWS the uncle knows something, and he isn't saying either, but for a totally different reason."

I stared at her. "Lollie, I have NO idea what you're talking about."

"Oh there's a surprise!" Brice imitated my voice again. "Our cute little airhead hasn't a clue what's going on!"

And suddenly my soul-mate went ballistic. "Will you two just stop!" she yelled. "I have totally had enough of being fought over like a bone!"

She glared at Brice. "You are driving me nuts!"

I felt a smug grin spreading over my face but my friend turned on me in a fury. "As for you, *carita*, you seem to have forgotten what angels are actually for."

"But I just—" I began.

"You don't get it, do you?" Lola shouted. "We're professionals, Boo. We can't let our personal business get in the way."

"But I just—" Brice began.

"I'm still talking actually," she told him. "Now here's the deal. You two go back to Uncle Noel's house to do some serious investigating. That should give you a chance to sort out your differences. I'm going to stay with Georgie. Is that clear?" she demanded.

"Crystal," we said nervously.

Brice and I beamed ourselves sulkily to Portman Square. We arrived just as Uncle Noel was going out for the evening, looking seriously spruced up and spiffy. He hailed a cab in Baker Street.

"Take me to Boodles in Marble Arch," he told the cabbie.

I was convinced this was some kind of Victorian strip joint, plus Brice and I were grimly ignoring each other, so I had a really nerve-wracking journey. I was incredibly relieved when Boodles turned out to be a respectable gentleman's club. Though personally I thought it could do with major refurbishing. The walls and ceilings had gone the colour of old tea from the constant puffing of cigars, and the rugs were so faded you couldn't even guess what colour they'd been.

We followed Uncle Noel upstairs into a smoky room full of Victorian gentlemen going "haw-haw-haw", like those depressing debates in the House of Commons. Some of the members had pulled their leather chairs into huddles to make it easier to chat. Others were lounging about with their feet on tables, or blatantly warming their backsides at the fire. They were all really old, like in their forties and fifties. And judging from the conversation about crown courts and plaintiffs and whatever, most of them were barristers like Georgie's uncle. I think a couple were even judges.

For the first hour or so, Uncle Noel circulated and made polite chit-chat like agony aunts tell you to do at parties. Then someone said, "Ah, Scrivener, tell us what you think about the stinking masses? Haw-haw-haw!"

This was so outrageous that I couldn't help catching Brice's eye. To my relief he didn't look away.

"They should put these guys in a museum for boring old bigots," he said.

"It's a shame we're not ghosts," I sighed. "At least we could play noughts and crosses on the mirror."

It was amazing! Those old buffers were so vile that Brice and I were actually bonding!

Brice gave me a grudging grin. "So how does Uncle Noel strike you, now he's in his natural habitat?"

"I think he seems totally ill at ease."

"That could be why he's drinking too much," said Brice.

"And have you noticed how that old guy with the sidewhiskers always pretends not to hear what he says?"

"Our Noel is a self-made man," explained Brice. "In their eyes, that makes him an upstart and a bounder."

The man with the sidewhiskers was thumping the table. "The urban poor breed like rabbits and we've got to put a stop to it!" He went into this long rant about the poor spreading their disgusting diseases, and pushing up crime rates. "By the end of the century we'll be overrun!"

Georgie's uncle seemed increasingly uncomfortable. "You all speak as if the poor are incapable of feeling as we do, as if they have no dreams or ambitions."

"That's true," I hissed to Brice. "The bit about them speaking, I mean, not the poor," I added hastily.

But old Sidewhiskers completely ignored Uncle Noel's outburst. "This so-called Whitechapel murderer is a prime example," he said. "The man's obviously a complete degenerate. I'd be very surprised if he even knows who his father was!"

I don't know if it was the old buffer's words or the approving haw-hawing that upset Georgie's uncle so much. Plus remember he'd really been knocking back the booze. But suddenly he just exploded with rage.

"Are you saying that a man has no right to better himself?" he burst out. "Must he then stay in the situation he was born to, no matter how degrading?"

"Dear, dear, we seem to have touched a raw nerve," someone muttered.

"Yet with education and a sincere desire to improve himself, a poor man can change beyond recognition!" Uncle Noel was almost shouting now. "Such a man might even come and mingle with you gentlemen in your precious club and you would be none the wiser!"

And dashing his glass to the floor he stormed downstairs and out into the street. We had to hurtle after him.

"I thought all Victorian guys were supposed to go in for stiff upper lips and repressing their feelings," I panted.

Georgie's uncle was barging drunkenly into other passers-by. He was so pickled that his thoughts were clearly audible. *I'm twice the man they are.*

No-one ever gave me so much as a helping hand. My father grudged every paltry penny he gave my mother. I was his by-blow, his bastard, so I had to make do with second best; a second-best school while my brother went to Eton, living in that poky house while they lived in luxury.

"Why is he so obsessed with his parents not being married?" I asked Brice. "Loads of my mates' parents weren't."

"It's different in these times," Brice explained. "If a Victorian was born on the wrong side of the blanket, he was considered to be disreputable, a really bad lot."

Georgie's uncle flagged down a passing hansom cab. We climbed into the high unsprung vehicle, with its smells of leather and horses, and went clipping through the foggy streets.

'Try harder, Noel,' Mama kept saying. Uncle Noel was still fuming to himself. *'Pass your exams, show him how clever you are, and you'll make your father proud of you.' There was no money to send me to university, so I worked as a legal clerk by day, and sat up all night studying for the bar. Papa will be proud of me when I get my articles, I thought.*

"Don't you feel just a *leetle* bit sorry for him?" I whispered.

Brice shook his head. "This guy is quite sorry enough for himself."

When we got back to Portman Square, Georgie's uncle went straight to his study and poured himself a generous glass of booze. Then he stumbled to a curtained alcove and pulled back the curtain. Behind it was a painting of a young fair-haired woman in a white dress.

"Haven't we seen her before somewhere?" Brice sounded puzzled.

"Omigosh," I gasped. "It's the woman in Georgie's locket!"

We stared at each other as this sank in. Then Brice gave an evil chuckle. "Well rock'n'roll! Uncle Noel had the hots for Georgie's mama!"

"Second best, always second best in everything." Uncle Noel was really working himself into a state. "Then I met you, Marguerite, and I thought my luck had changed."

He went on rambling drunkenly about how he'd loved Georgie's mama at first sight, but he was poor and illegitimate so he hadn't dared approach her.

"Perhaps you could have grown to love me," Uncle Noel sniffled. "But before I could pluck up courage to speak, my half-brother stole you away from me."

Brice's eyes widened. "Oh – that could be a motive!"

The uncle opened a drawer and took out a framed miniature of the widowed Marguerite with her two small children. I was startled to see they were both wearing dresses!

"Oh my poor darling," he groaned. "Little Georgina gets more like you every time I see her."

My mouth dropped open. Georgina! NO way!

No wonder him mum had put him in a dress. Tough streetwise cigar-smoking Georgie was really a girl!!!

I saw Brice's smug expression and realised he'd known all along.

"You rat!" I said. "Why didn't you say something?"

"I knew you'd figure it out eventually," he grinned.

The door opened and a tiny woman came in, wearing a full-length nightdress and a prim little bedcap with trailing ribbons. "Do try to control yourself, dearest," she said sharply. "The servants will hear."

Uncle Noel's wife might have been pocket-sized, but she was totally deadly. The room was suddenly crackling with ruthless vibes.

Her husband guiltily went to cover the portrait, but Aunt Agnes smiled. "I am not jealous of your Marguerite, beloved," she said with poisonous sweetness. "For she is dead and I am very much alive."

"You are indeed a formidable woman!" He tried to embrace her but tiny Aunt Agnes ducked neatly under his arm.

"Formidable, some might even say 'frightening'," she quoted.

"My love, I didn't mean – have you been spying on me, Agnes?" he asked in dismay.

"You bet your life she has," Brice muttered.

"Purely for your own good," Aunt Agnes said calmly. "You lack the necessary steel to follow our plan through to its conclusion. Luckily I am strong enough for us both."

"But when I think of Marguerite's daughter ending her days among drunks and pickpockets," he blubbered. "I have such nightmares, Agnes...!"

"It's only seeing her which upsets you," she interrupted swiftly. "Once the brats are out of harm's way, you'll feel better."

I heard Brice breathe in sharply.

"I bet she's got a fur coat made from baby Dalmatians, don't you?" I whispered.

Aunt Agnes poured them both a drink and raised her glass to the portrait.

"Silly girl!" she said in musing voice. "She might still be alive if she had married you. Indeed, dearest, she would have married you, if it hadn't been for your half-brother's selfishness. Wasn't it enough that he stood to inherit the law firm and all your father's money? Did he have to break your heart too?"

"Georgie's right. She *is* a witch!" said Brice.

"He was so cold and cruel that he left me no choice. I had to become cruel just like him, or go under," Uncle Noel sniffled.

Aunt Agnes gave a low chuckle. "But what a sweet moment it must have been, when you saw that proud old man standing in the dock like a common criminal."

I was shocked. She was shamelessly manipulating him, constantly reminding him how he'd suffered, trying to make him feel like this money was actually *owing* to him.

Uncle Noel gave her a watery smile. "Yes, yes, a very sweet moment."

"And the ripples go on and on. First your father's public shame, then your brother discovering that the man he so worshipped was a liar and a thief.

They died broken men, Noel. They tried to destroy you but you broke them!"

"But my brother suffered for so many years before he died, and then Marguerite—" he began.

"Don't interrupt, dearest," she said coldly. "The force of your revenge has reverberated through three generations of Hannays. It needs only one more act of courage, and they'll be gone for ever. Then all your father's money will be ours."

"But what if someone finds out? I had my own father accused of embezzling...!"

"Who is going to tell?" she said contemptuously. "Not that fool Edwin Godbolt. He is terrified you will harm his sister. And the man who forged those false documents, Alfred Rose—"

"Lilly," her husband corrected her. "Alfred Lilly."

"Lilly is in the Union Workhouse, and the matron says he has only days to live. That leaves Lovelace, and by now that old villain is either dead or committing new felonies on the other side of the world. For all we know he died of typhus on the transport ship, like your father."

Uncle Noel gazed at his wife with a kind of awe. "You make everything seem so simple, my love."

"But it is dearest, it is," Aunt Agnes said triumphantly. "Wonderfully and exquisitely simple!"

They left the room arm in arm, leaving me and Brice totally stunned.

I gulped. "This isn't just a field trip any more, is it?"

"No," he said.

"It's a mission, isn't it?"

"Yes."

CHAPTER EIGHT

"Let's get out of here," said Brice. "This house gives me the chills."

I naturally headed for the door. Brice grabbed my arm impatiently. "You will keep forgetting you're an angel!" And he pulled me through the wall into the cold dark street outside.

Melanie, that was so groovy – you just shimmered through a wall! I told myself. It was actually quite a cool sensation.

Brice was still ranting. "And that aunt is pure evil. Her husband practically destroyed an entire family and she's just cheering him on to the finishing post!"

I gulped. "She was talking like she wanted him to make them, you know, disappear."

"Noel Scrivener knows some unsavoury Victorians," he said grimly. "It wouldn't be hard for him to find someone to bump his nieces off, no questions asked."

"We should go back and tell Lollie and start figuring out what to do," I said.

I saw Brice's expression change at the mention of Lola. "Actually, I could do with a few minutes to get my head together."

"Oh, that's OK," I said hastily, "I'll beam back by myself."

To my surprise, he said, "No, don't rush off. Let's just walk around the square for a bit, see how the rich live."

It was well past midnight and the square was almost deserted. Outside one brightly lit house a coachman was dozing in his coach, waiting for someone to finish socialising inside. Most of the windows were dark. The fog had practically gone, there were just drifty veils here and there, but the air felt damp and raw. After a while I noticed Brice shivering in his T-shirt.

"You don't have to freeze, or did you forget you're an angel?" I teased.

"Oh, yeah." He genuinely hadn't noticed.

I could see this struggle going on inside him. He

seemed desperate to get something off his chest, and suddenly he just blurted it out. "I was just trying to take care of her. Guys are supposed to do that. Then she accuses me of acting like a dog with a bone!" He swallowed. "Was that how I seemed to you?"

"Do you want the honest truth?" I asked.

"Well, I certainly don't want you to lie," he said scathingly.

"Well, you have been acting a bit possessive." I took a breath. "We both have."

Babe, what are you doing? I thought. You almost apologised to Brice!

Just then a little grey cat came running up to us. Reuben is teaching me this cool angel language which is understood by practically all animals, so I petted her and tried out my phrases.

I noticed Brice darting sideways glances at me. Suddenly he said, "I think I'm a bit out of my depth with this boy-girl business."

"Hey, hold it right there," I said nervously. "Is this going to get embarrassing? Because if so I'm beaming out of here pronto."

He grinned. "I'm not going to ask you about the angels and the bees. It's boy-girl feelings I'm having trouble with."

I shrugged. "Yeah well, you're a guy. What can I say?"

"I wish that's all it was," he said. "Mel, can you even imagine what my life was like before the Agency took me back? I've been hanging out with some really dark characters, you know. I feel like one of those kids raised by wolves, except with me it was demons and ghouls."

"I know! It must have been a total nightmare." I pulled an embarrassed face. "That sounded really dumb. You're right. I can't even imagine what the Hell dimensions are like. I don't know how you survived."

"I don't know if I did, not totally," he admitted. "But Lola seems to think – she's so amazing, isn't she?"

"She's the best," I said softly.

"I guess I got a bit carried away." He took a deep breath. "Sorry if I acted like a jerk."

"Yeah well, I wasn't exactly behaving like an angel." I paused and shook my head. "Did I really say that?"

I held out my hand to show him it was starting to rain. "Have you finished soul-searching now? Because I am dying to see Lollie's face when we tell her Georgie is actually a girl!"

Back at The Three Cripples, we found a truly touching scene. Georgie was curled up on the floor fast asleep, cuddling the ugly dog for comfort. Around her in a protective circle were dozens of raidiant little globes of rose-coloured light.

Lola had been reading her Angel Handbook while Georgie was sleeping. When we came in, she whipped off her glasses, smiling. "Hi."

"Pink lights," said Brice. "That's nice."

I knew he was thinking, pink for a girl.

"I thought they'd help him feel safe," Lollie explained.

"Help *her* feel safe," I corrected demurely.

Lola's eyes widened. "*She*? Omigosh, you're kidding!"

"It's true," said Brice. "Young Georgie Hannay here is actually Georgina. You can't blame her for disguising herself as a boy, living on the streets and with the Ripper on the loose."

We scrutinised Georgie's face by the glow of Lola's angel lights.

"I can't imagine how I ever thought she was a boy," I whispered.

Lola shook her head in wonder. "That's one brave little human."

I went to sit by the hearth where a few embers

still gave out heat. "Brice knew straight off," I said in a casual voice.

I saw my sharp-eyed friend register that Brice and I had made a truce, but she just said, "So what else did you guys find out?"

We explained how Georgie's uncle had developed this major grudge because his favoured half-brother had married the girl he loved.

"So Scrivener decided to take revenge on the entire Hannay family," said Brice. "He used his dodgy contacts to acquire forged 'evidence' that would make it seem as if his hugely well-respected old man, Charles Hannay, had embezzled his clients' money. It was obviously a brilliant forgery, because the judge sentenced him to be transported – only he died of typhus before he reached Australia. Are you going to eat all that trail mix, Mel?"

"Oh, no, sorry!" I took over the story while Brice munched.

"It looks like Georgie's papa never got over the shame of having his father publicly humiliated. He and Marguerite eventually had kids, but I think the foundations of his world had like, crumbled." It was only now I was explaining it to Lola that I totally understood this.

"So Georgie's dad gradually gave up the ghost

and died of a broken heart," said Brice. "And a few years later, their mama followed."

Lola shook her head. "So Uncle Scrivener is indirectly responsible for these kids being orphaned."

"He's *totally* responsible." Brice sounded furious. "Not only that, he makes it seem as if Georgie's parents left their two little girls destitute. Then this guy has the nerve to whinge about having nightmares!"

"Someone must have known what was going on," Lola said.

"Yeah, Edwin Godbolt, who was conveniently sent to gaol for a crime he didn't commit," said Brice. "Also Scrivener's threatened his sister, so while she's still alive, he can't tell what he knows."

"There's one other witness," I reminded him. "That old forger, Alfred Lilly. But the aunt said he could pop off any minute." I yanked at my hair. "It's SO frustrating being invisible. If we could just materialise for five tiny minutes we could go to Scotland Yard—"

"No way!" Lola said sternly. "Last time you pulled that stunt you almost got expelled."

Brice looked interested. "Why haven't I heard this story?"

"Omigosh," I shrieked. "OMIGOSH, guys! I know what we're going to do!!"

I was so overexcited, I literally had to fan myself with both hands before I could get the words out. "We'll go to Minerva's first thing and Brice can ask his spirit buddies to tell Georgie and Charlotte what their evil rellies are up to. If the girls can get to Alfred Lilly in time, he can maybe make this like, deathbed confession to the cops or whatever." I beamed at them. "Well, what do you think?"

"I'm grudgingly impressed," Brice admitted.

I blew on my nails. "Not bad for an airhead, huh?"

"It'll mean giving Georgie a cosmic nudge," said Lola. "She might have her own plans."

Brice emptied the last of my trail mix into his mouth. "Sweetheart, if the Agency wanted to play it by the rules, why would they send *us*?"

Lola and Brice started swapping trouble-shooting stories, but I moved closer to the fire, staring into the dying embers.

Brice had made it sound like this had always been a mission, a mission that just happened to be in educational disguise. This bothered me, because deep down I knew I'd let Georgie down. Not only had I allowed my personal business to get in the way, but I'd deliberately distanced myself from her. Georgie's life was unbelievably tragic and I hadn't been able to stand the thought of how painful it must be. So to protect myself, I'd made her into this quirky little Victorian character I was studying for a project.

But now I took a proper look at Georgie, I mean really looked at her vulnerable sleeping face, and I thought, in another life she could be me and I could be her.

And you know what? I felt really moved to think that after all my stupid mistakes, I'd been given another chance to help her.

Then I thought – omigosh, how karmic is that! Like, before I could help Georgie, I had to learn all this heavy stuff about myself. And *then* I thought, it's true what they say about the Agency. It does move in mysterious ways.

Next morning, Georgie had dark circles under her eyes. She was so exhausted she could hardly drag her clothes on.

"Have you got somewhere safe to sleep tonight, dearie?" the landlady of The Cripples asked her anxiously.

"I've got dozens of places I can go," Georgie boasted, but I felt her terror go through me like a blade. Because since her mama died, she didn't have anywhere safe to go, not tonight, not ever.

It was wet and windy outside and Georgie had to stop on the doorstep to turn up her collar. Two grim-faced bobbies stood guarding the alleyway, where the girl had been murdered.

It made me shudder to think that we'd been in the next street when it happened. We should have helped her, I thought miserably. What's the use of being an angel if you can't save someone's life? And then I thought, but we can still save Georgie.

Georgie didn't need nudging in the direction of Milkwell Street. She went there all by herself. The poor kid had totally lost all her confidence and didn't know where else to go. She managed to keep it together, up to the moment when Ivy opened the door, and then she burst into tears, babbling hysterically about her brush with the Ripper. Charlotte came running, wide-eyed.

"I can't do this any more, Charlie," Georgie sobbed. "What's going to happen to me?"

Her sister looked genuinely scared. She was used to Georgie being the strong one. "Tell us exactly what happened," she said bravely.

Minerva appeared in the kitchen doorway. "Is something wrong?" she asked. Several concerned-looking spirits followed her in. Brice immediately nipped over to do a bit of cosmic networking.

"I hope you don't mind Georgie being here, Miss Temple. He didn't know where else to go." Charlotte sounded flustered.

I saw a spirit say something to Minerva, and she made a sound of genuine dismay. "I am being told that someone has been menacing this child," she said anxiously. "Have you any idea who it might be?"

"Oh, yes, Miss Temple," said Charlotte. "A poor girl was killed in Whitechapel last night, and the Ripper ran right past Georgie in the street."

Minerva shuddered. "I'm not talking about that fiend in human form. This is someone close to you, someone who did you both a great wrong many years ago. You pose a threat to this person and you are in very great danger."

Georgie backed away, with the tears still trickling down her face. "I've heard about your seances," she burst out. "All those levers and pulleys and ectoplasm and I don't want nothing, anything I mean, to do with any of your 'spirits'."

Charlotte flinched, obviously fearing she would lose her job, but Minerva just settled herself into a chair.

"Now listen to me, dear," she said. "I will not deny that I have occasionally contrived a few atmospheric effects to further my own ends."

"You cheated people," said Georgie, who was so upset that she had totally forgotten to be polite to her elders and betters.

"Yes I did," said Minerva. "Maybe I should have trusted the spirit world to take care of me, but I was afraid of – well, never mind what I was afraid of. But you must believe me, child. The spirits have been talking to me ever since I can remember, and they are insisting that someone intends to harm you and Charlotte. And stop pretending you're not listening, Ivy," she added calmly. "We're going to hold a little private seance for these girls."

Georgie sounded frightened. "Why did you call me that? I'm not a girl."

Minerva clicked her tongue. "It's not like the spirits to slip up about something like that!" She smiled into Georgie's eyes. "I know this must be upsetting, dearie. But I think we should know what kind of villain we're dealing with."

I could see Georgie still didn't believe in Minerva's powers, but she was too shattered to argue.

All the humans sat at the kitchen table and held hands, slightly awkwardly because of the table being square. All the invisible beings stood around them, with our angel contingent standing close to Georgie.

With our help, Minerva described the big house where the Hannays used to live, and how they used to go flying kites on Hampstead Heath, until Georgie's dad's nerves got so bad he stopped going out at all.

"Charlotte could have told you that," Georgie growled.

"That's true," Minerva agreed.

"Ask Georgie why she was looking at that silver locket in the lamplight," I said impulsively. I felt a zing of cosmic electricity as Minerva heard my words.

"But she didn't tell me about you standing under that street lamp last night, gazing at that silver locket," Minerva said smoothly. She smiled at the stunned Georgie. "Thought you were all alone in the world, didn't you? Well, you aren't, you see."

Georgie was making little gasping sounds, as if she might be crying.

"You think I'm talking about my spirits, don't you?" said Minerva. "But I'm not."

"Who then?" whispered Georgie.

"Angels, lovie," Minerva told her. "You've got three angels standing behind you now. I can't see them, but I know they're there."

Tears spilled down Georgie's face. "I want to believe you," she wept, "I really do. But I don't know if I can!"

"Do you need a tissue?" Lola whispered.

"No, I'm fine," I sniffled.

My plan was succeeding beyond my wildest dreams. After we hit Georgie with the locket message, she became a total believer. She was naturally distressed to hear that a dark-haired male relative, with the initials N.S., intended to harm her and her sister. But as it sank in, Georgie seemed strangely relieved, as if the pieces of a confusing puzzle were finally coming together.

"Some nights, I'd be trying to sleep in a doorway, and I'd tell myself stories to help myself drift off. I'd imagine how Uncle Noel would come riding up in a hansom, telling me he didn't care what Aunt Agnes said, he was going to have us to live with him." The memory made Georgie turn red with shame. "But when I was with him, he'd always make me feel all mixed up inside. He'd seem so kind, but then he'd deliberately say things to hurt me, as if he wanted to punish me for some reason."

She clutched at her sister. "What is he going to do to us, Charlie? I'm really scared."

This was our cue to tell Minerva about Alfred Lilly. The spirits relayed the relevant info, and to start with everything went like a dream. Then Georgie said eagerly, "So where can we find this old forger?"

I saw Minerva's eyes cloud over. "I'm not sure," she said in an anxious voice. "The spirits seem to be fading away."

The spirits turned to each other in a panic, like: well, I'm sure I'm not fading. Are you fading?

"She's blocking," hissed Brice.

Omigosh, I thought, what are we going to do if she won't give Georgie the message?

And then I remembered. Minerva Temple, the successful medium, had once been Minnie Tuttle, a defenceless workhouse child. Apparently her experiences had scarred her so deeply that she couldn't even hear a message that had the word 'workhouse' in it. Without thinking I moved round to Minerva's side of the table and put my arms around her.

"Don't be scared," I whispered. "Those workhouse people hurt you because they were bigger than you and you were young and helpless, but now it's these little girls who need help."

I hadn't actually given any thought to the effect an angelic hug might have on a gifted psychic, but let me tell you, it was pure dynamite! Minerva shot out of her trance like a rocket.

"Charlotte, fetch your coat and bonnet," she said briskly. "It's bitterly cold out. I don't want you setting off that cough."

Charlotte was bewildered. "But you didn't tell us where the old man lives?"

Minerva had started rummaging on the kitchen dresser. "The worst place this side of Hell, lovie," she told her.

I heard the dread in Georgie's voice. "You mean the Union Workhouse."

"I vowed I'd never go back," said Minerva, still rummaging among the bottles and jars. "But the spirit world has other plans." She found a green bottle, uncorked it and took a good swig.

"Dutch courage," she said bravely. "Now I'm ready to meet this old rascal. And if he has any breath left in his body, he's going to tell me everything he knows!"

CHAPTER NINE

The Union Workhouse was actually several grim small-windowed buildings, set behind tall iron gates like an army garrison. On the other side of the gates, I glimpsed drab figures listlessly sweeping paths in the drizzle.

"They make them wear uniform," I whispered. "Like prison."

Brice's tone was savage. "This *is* prison, for people tried and found guilty of being poor. Can you believe husbands and wives have to live in separate parts of the workhouse? The authorities let them meet up on Sundays if they're good."

I understood now why Minerva hadn't dared to rely on the spirit world to keep the money rolling in.

She was terrified of falling back into the grey Hell dimension of the workhouse.

An expressionless porter let us in through the gates. We had collected a police constable on the way, a stout fatherly man, and seeing Minerva falter, he immediately took charge and asked where they could find the matron.

The porter silently pointed out a path leading to one of the staff cottages.

A scared little maid in a badly-fitting workhouse gown showed us in. The matron had been having her elevenses: cold roast beef, pickled onions and a pint of porter to wash it down. She listened with growing astonishment as the constable explained that they needed to talk to one of the workhouse inmates. "We have reason to believe Mr Lilly has vital information about a serious miscarriage of justice," he said solemnly.

She gave an outraged snort. "I don't care how serious it is. My inmates follow an orderly routine and I can't allow them to be disrupted."

But the policeman stood his ground, telling her that if she didn't cooperate, he would have to charge her with obstructing the due process of the law, and the matron eventually gave in.

"Though how a senile old man can help you with

your inquiries, I don't know!" she said spitefully. "He don't know what day of the week it is, most of the time."

We were so proud of Minerva. As she walked into the dreadful institution she'd vowed never to enter again, she looked totally composed. No, better than composed. She looked like a queen. The echoey bile-green corridors and those nauseating whiffs from the kitchens must have seemed like a bad recurring dream, yet her face showed no trace of the childhood terrors churning underneath. "We'll just be a few minutes," she told the girls reassuringly. "We'll be outside in the fresh air in no time."

"We will if that matron woman's got anything to with it," muttered Brice.

Keen to finish her morning snack, the matron was rushing her visitors through the wards.

One room still stands out in my memory. It had a smell I associate with shipyards, and you could hardly see the inmates at first because the air was bewilderingly full of tiny floating fibres. Men in skimpy workhouse coats and trousers were sitting around a vast table, patiently teasing apart strands from apparently endless coils of industrial-type rope. All the wards were unheated and their fingers, already raw and blistered from the ropes, were blue with cold.

"It's called 'picking oakum'," Brice whispered. "The idea is that people aren't supposed to get something for nothing. They have to earn their bowl of watered-down gruel, otherwise everyone will want to come. Joke," he added quickly.

You'll think I'm dense but until then I genuinely hadn't realised why they called it a 'workhouse'.

We never saw the children's ward and I was grateful. Georgie and Charlotte totally didn't need to go through that.

At the far end of the very last ward was the door to the infirmary. I saw Minerva and the policeman brace themselves before they entered, so I was already expecting the worst.

I'm sorry, but there are no words which adequately describe the horror of that ward. It was a place of pure despair. Inmates were only brought here when they became so ill that it was pointless trying to squeeze any more work out of them; when they were on the brink of death, basically. Many were so ravaged by illness that if it wasn't for their clothes, you couldn't have said if they were male or female. You could hardly even tell they were human.

I was deeply grateful to Mr Allbright for teaching us a new technique ideal for use in this type of harrowing situation, when you can't stop and help each human individually. You connect with your cosmic energy source and command, "Stream!" and immediately uplifting celestial vibes stream out of you to everyone who needs it. OK, so it's not much, but like Reuben always says, better to light one candle than to curse the dark.

The matron stopped beside an iron bedstead. "Well here he is," she announced. "And much good may it do you," she muttered as she bustled away.

We all looked down at the shrunken old man under the faded quilt.

Brice shook his head. "Damn. Too late."

"I felt it as soon as we came in," Lola sighed.

When a human is getting ready to leave the Earth, there is an unmistakable vibe; a kind of intense, almost unbearable, sweetness.

"Mr Lilly," the policeman was saying doggedly. "We need to ask you a few questions. Have you ever had any connection with a gentlemen called Noel Scrivener?"

Minerva shook her head. "He can't hear you."

The policeman sounded offended. "He's responding to my voice."

The old man's watery unfocused eyes had widened with surprise. He broke into a tremulous smile, and we heard his thoughts. *I can die happy now. I'll never get to Heaven, old sinner that I am, but now I've seen the angels, I can die happy.*

Brice's expression was unreadable. "This is just incredible."

"I know," I said sympathetically. "I hate how they teach humans that stuff, about having to be good to get into Heaven."

"Actually I was talking about Agency timing," Brice explained. "Here's an old man dying alone, scared he's too wicked to get to Heaven. Now suddenly there are three angels in the vicinity. How do they do it?"

Lola was stroking the old man's knobbly hand. "Forget about the past, *amigo mio*," she whispered lovingly. "Let it go. Focus on what happens next." My friend trusts her instincts more than any angel I know, and she had instantly recognised what we had to do.

I knew we were just about to lose our one witness to Noel Scrivener's crime, but that seemed suddenly irrelevant. Like getting born, dying is intense for everyone involved. There's just no room to think about anything else.

There was a beautiful moment when the

forgotten angel inside Alfred Lilly finally slipped free and stood beside the old man's worn-out body. And suddenly the room filled with luminous figures who had come to guide him to the next world.

"I'm glad we could help him die in peace," Lola whispered.

"Me too," I whispered back. "I just wish we'd got there sooner so we could have talked to him. Then those poor girls could have got what's rightfully theirs."

Minerva gently closed the corpse's eyes. Her voice was full of sorrow. "He's gone," she told the girls. "I'm so sorry."

I was sorry too, but I was also mesmerised by what was happening to the spirit of Alfred Lilly, who seemed to be getting younger every minute. His face lit up with joy as he recognised the old friends and relations who had come to meet him.

"Hope you really enjoy Heaven, Mr Lilly," I whispered.

The forger turned to smile at me. "Lovelace," he said clearly, and he touched his chest. "The letter's in his pocket."

And he'd gone, leaving me in a blur of astonishment.

Lovelace. That was the name of the villain Aunt Agnes believed had died on the transport ship to Australia; Noel Scrivener's accomplice!

Scenes flashed before my eyes at lightning speed. Red dirt, pink cartoon birds, silver eucalyptus trees and an ex-convict with a guilty secret. *I put it in my pocket, I put it in my pocket...*

Omigosh, I thought. OMIGOSH!! Because I suddenly knew exactly how Sherlock Holmes felt when he solved a case.

Mr Lilly had just given me the crucial information we needed to restore Georgie and Charlotte's stolen fortune. And it totally didn't worry me that our witness was on the other side of the world, in the middle of the red Martian desert of the Northern Territories. Because when you're in full angel mode, you just know with every shimmery angelic cell that miracles can happen.

"*Carita?*" said Lola anxiously. "Are you all right?"

"I'm better than all right," I burbled. "I might even be a genius!"

I turned to Brice. "Do you think your spirit buddies would do us one final favour?"

*   *   *

OK, I admit to a bad moment when Ivy showed the Scotland Yard detectives into Minerva's parlour. But it was just a bad moment.

We had seances down by this time. First we softened them up with titbits of relatively trivial personal info; the name of one detective's favourite childhood dog, that time the other detective nicked money from his mama's purse and blamed it on the gardener's boy.

After that the cops became a great deal more open-minded and listened to our revelations with increasingly attentive expressions. The younger one was taking notes laboriously. "So your, erm, spirits think Mr Scrivener's accomplice may have been transported to Australia?"

With the help of her team of angelic researchers, Minerva gave a detailed description of the area where we'd found the old convict, including the sacred rock and the mission house.

The detectives were sufficiently perturbed by what they heard to pay a visit to Uncle Noel's house that afternoon, taking Charlotte and Georgie with them. Naturally we tagged along.

When Uncle Noel saw the girls' accusing faces, it was like a dam burst inside him. He cracked and tearfully confessed what he'd done. As Brice said later, Uncle Noel just wasn't cut out to be a villain. He wanted all the perks, but he wanted to be Mister Nice Guy at the same time. No wonder he made Georgie feel so confused!

The next twenty-four hours brought all kinds of satisfying changes for the Hannay girls. Scotland Yard sent a telegram to the cops in Alice Springs, asking them to track down a transported criminal called Sid Lovelace for questioning. And Edwin Godbolt was released from Newgate. Can you believe that old sweetheart immediately came round to Minerva's house to volunteer to be the children's legal adviser, for free? He brought his twin sister too. She looked exactly like him, except for being female.

There was quite a party by that time. The two detectives had popped back, with a police photographer. I think he was hoping to capture Minerva's spirits on one of his photographic plates.

I remember looking around the parlour and just feeling so honoured to be part of this happy ending.

"It's so cool that Minerva wants the girls to come and live with her," I said to Lola.

My friend was watching Brice chatting to his see-thru buddies in the corner. "Wouldn't you love to know how he learned to speak Spook?" she grinned. "Now that has to be a good story!"

Suddenly Lollie's face took on a listening expression. "I can't believe it's that time already!" she groaned. "I was just getting into the Victorians."

I couldn't believe it either, but when the Agency want you to move on, they totally let you know about it.

"This is so unfair," I complained. "I mean, I know things will work out but I wanted to SEE them work out."

Brice looked over. "You still can, you ditzy angel," he called. "And when we get back I'll prove it to you."

Then the entire parlour lit up and we blasted off back to our heavenly home.

"There'd better be a very good reason for dragging us down to the Angel Watch Centre at this hour," I yawned.

I'd been hoping for a nice lie-in the next morning. Instead we were tiptoeing past flickering booths where AW personnel were working vigilantly at their computers.

Brice let us into a private cubicle usually reserved for Agency staff. "Stop moaning, Beeby." He slid a glittering disk into the machine.

A screen lit up and a familiar scene appeared; red dirt and eucalyptus trees wavering in a heat haze.

"I can't believe you were able to swing this!" Lollie gasped.

He tapped his nose. "Inside information," he said smugly.

Somehow Brice had acquired one of the cosmic recordings the Agency uses for training purposes. From an angelic point of view, Earth's past, present and future all occur simultaneously. So it was technically possible for us all to see what had happened after the telegram arrived at the police station in Alice Springs.

We watched in total silence as Aussie cops in sun helmets finally tracked Sid Lovelace down at the mission house. The missionaries must have taken pity on him after all. Lola and I gasped as the old man, still weak from fever, reached into his pocket and pulled out a letter so old it had almost disintegrated. The writing was only just visible, but after Brice had enhanced the image, we just made out the incriminating passage requesting Alfred Lilly to falsify certain legal documents. At the bottom of the letter was a signature. *Noel Scrivener*

Lovelace handed the letter to the police, and I felt the terrible weight roll off him, like the lifting of a curse.

This is SO cosmic, I thought. We saved him, and now he's saved Georgie and Charlotte, so he can start to forgive himself.

"That's it. Show's over!" Brice said brusquely. "I'd better get this back before anyone notices."

Lola and I agreed to meet up with him later at Guru. By this time we were totally wide awake and extremely peckish.

"Do you believe he actually stole that disk?" Lola giggled as we breezed into our favourite breakfast hang-out. "The guy's a total maverick!"

"I'll say. I'd love to know what he was up to that night, when he left us with those kids."

Lola's expression changed. "Actually, Boo, I do know, but you've got to promise not to tell him I told you."

I was covered in shame when Lollie told me that Brice had gone to help the spirit of one of the Ripper's victims. The poor girl had been so traumatised that she needed angelic assistance to help her cross over to the Next World.

"Why ever didn't he say?" I exclaimed.

"I guess he thought you wouldn't believe him," Lola said. "You do tend to be a bit hard on him."

And suddenly Lola and I were having our first proper conversation in months. I told her how jealous I'd been when I realised she and Brice were together, and she was astonished.

"Together! We're not 'together', Boo! No way! He needed a friend and I really like bad boys, OK? Babe, you're my soul-mate! I wouldn't drop you for some – guy!"

I was stunned. "Like, you didn't ever kiss?"

Lola gave a wicked giggle. "Now, did I say that? It gets v. romantic under the stars, you know!"

We were still having a giggly heart-to-heart over our breakfast pastries when Brice came in with Reuben and his bizarre mate Chase. "Brice has been showing us a picture of your Minerva," Reuben beamed. I got the funny feeling he knew something we didn't.

"Don't ruin my story," objected Brice. "I found a book on Victorian mediums and there she was. She became quite famous. Here's a picture."

Time is so weird. It seemed like only yesterday when that photograph was taken, and in my time scheme it was. Yet here it was in a book written more than a century later, by a sceptical academic who thought all mediums were frauds and charlatans.

The black and white portrait showed Minerva looking v. stern and Victorian. Light seemed to have leaked into the camera, inadvertently creating some weirdly extraterrestrial-type FX.

I stared at the three featureless blobs beside her. The photographer had snapped us at the exact moment we beamed back to Heaven.

"This is my favourite bit!" Brice pointed to the caption.

"Minerva Temple and her angelic advisers," I read. "The heavenly trio famously helped Scotland Yard solve the notorious Scrivener case." Underneath the author had written, "An obvious fake."

We all howled with laughter. It is so cool to be back, I thought. This is one of the happiest moments of my life!

"So what was it like, going on a mission with your evil nemesis, Mel?" asked Chase.

The entire café went silent. Chase, otherwise known as Mowgli, mostly hangs out with the animal kingdom and is not known for his tact. I really wished the ground would open up and swallow me. Everyone was staring at me, waiting to hear my answer. I felt my face grow bright red.

"Well, actually—" I began.

I stopped. This matters, Melanie, I thought. It matters what you say here. Don't wriggle out of it.

Don't try to please anybody. Just answer him truthfully.

Brice was trying to look as if he didn't care what I thought.

I forced myself to meet his eyes.

"It was educational," I said finally. "Unexpectedly educational."

Coming soon in the brilliant **ANGELS UNLIMITED** series...

Fighting Fit

Mel gets the gladiator groove!

Mel's big-time crush Orlando's got a lot on his mind. So when he puts together a team of angel volunteers to go to Ancient Rome, Mel signs up. Hey, it's a chance to get close to the boy of her dreams! But in the cruel, decadent world of the Roman Empire's last days, her fantasies crumble. Who is the mysterious girl gladiator Orlando is trying so hard to protect? Is his concern purely professional, or is it something more?

Join Mel in her sixth cosmic adventure!

An imprint of HarperCollins*Publishers*

Also coming soon – www.angelsunlimited.co.uk!

Read the **ANGELS UNLIMITED** book that started it all!

Winging it

Mel is on a mission...

Mel isn't your average angel. How would you feel if you wound up in a posh Angel Academy, learning about halos and teamwork, when all you're really interested in is shopping and boys? Her angel wardrobe is drop-dead gorgeous, admittedly. But hey, if she's an angel, she should look divine, right? It's just all the work that really freaks her out. But when Mel goes on her first angelic assignment to wartime London, she realises that maybe, for the first time, she's found something she's actually good at...

Join Mel in her first cosmic adventure!

An imprint of HarperCollins*Publishers*

Also coming soon – www.angelsunlimited.co.uk!

Order Form

To order direct from the publishers, just make a list of the titles you want and fill in the form below:

Name ....

Address ....

....

....

Send to: Dept 6, HarperCollins Publishers Ltd, Westerhill Road, Bishopbriggs, Glasgow G64 2QT.

Please enclose a cheque or postal order to the value of the cover price, plus:

UK & BFPO: Add £1.00 for the first book, and 25p per copy for each additional book ordered.

Overseas and Eire: Add £2.95 service charge. Books will be sent by surface mail but quotes for airmail despatch will be given on request.

A 24-hour telephone ordering service is available to holders of Visa, MasterCard, Amex or Switch cards on 0141- 772 2281.

An imprint of HarperCollins*Publishers*